Mr. Jer

Vol. 3

B. M. Croker

Alpha Editions

This edition published in 2023

ISBN : 9789357952781

Design and Setting By
Alpha Editions
www.alphaedis.com
Email - info@alphaedis.com

Contents

CHAPTER XXX.
WHAT PEOPLE SAID—ESPECIALLY WHAT TWO PEOPLE SAID.

When Mark Jervis came all eagerness to claim his supper dance from Miss Gordon, he saw at once that something was wrong. The merry smile—her greatest charm—he sought in vain upon her face; her expression was grave, almost stern. She was actually looking at him as if he was an absolute stranger. *She knew!*

He glanced quickly at her partner, and the mystery was instantly solved. Yes, he recollected the man's goggling blue eyes. Where had he seen him? Where? The cordial accost—

"Hallo, Jervis! Came out with you in the *Victoria*!" promptly dispelled his last hope.

"Yes, so you did," nodding. "Glad to see you here to-night. I suppose you have been globe-trotting, like the rest of us!"

"*You* have not done much trotting, by all accounts, of late."

"No, not much," rather shortly. Then, to Honor, "This is our waltz."

She gazed at him for an instant in haughty silence, then she answered—

"Yes; but I don't think I shall dance, thank you."

"Oh do," he urged, as the stranger moved off. "Let us have just one dance. After the dance—the deluge! I see you know. We can have that out later on—but *don't* let us miss this."

The young lady was passionately fond of dancing, the floor, the inspiriting waltz, a first-rate partner, proved too tempting—"Yes," she said to herself, "just one last waltz, and then—the deluge." Not one word did she utter when they halted for a few seconds. She kept her face purposely averted, and appeared to find an absorbing interest in other people. When they once more launched into the vortex, it appeared to him that she did not dance with her usual buoyancy and light-heartedness. She was as stiff and as rigid as a china doll—apparently she shrank from the support of a millionaire's arm—his embrace was contamination. At last the waltz was over, every one was streaming out, and they naturally followed the crowd. They passed Mrs. Brande, concealing (she fondly believed) enormous yawns behind a black transparent fan; they passed Mrs. Langrishe, issuing bulletins of Sir Gloster's condition to several interested matrons. They went through the verandah side by side, down the steps, and were brought up at last by the rustic railing overlooking the gardens and tennis-court. It was a warm moonlight night, bright as day, and breathlessly still. Dozens of other couples were strolling, standing, or sitting about in the open air, even the chaperons had come forth (a new and in some instances fatal departure) to taste the sweets of a June night in the Himalayas.

Before their eyes rose the long range of snows—India's white crown; beneath them lay the gardens—a jungle of dew-steeped roses, tall lilies, and great shrubs of heliotrope. Balsac declares that perfume reminds more vividly than words; be that as it may, the slightest perfume of heliotrope invariably recalled that scene and hour to Honor Gordon's memory.

"So I see that it has all come out!" began Jervis, intrepidly, on the principle that the first blow is half the battle, "and that you know."

"Yes"—turning slowly to face him—"and no thanks to you, Mr. Jervis."

"Of course you are awfully angry with me. Nearly" (oh, most unfortunate speech!) "as angry as you were with that imp the day you tore up her picture."

"I am not exactly angry," she replied with tremulous dignity. "Why should I be angry? I am merely enlightened. I know who is who now. I dare say you found the little game of deceiving every one most entertaining. You seem to have quite a genius for playing a double part."

"You are awfully rough on me," he interrupted. "But I suppose I deserve it."

"Now I have but one character, such as it is, so I cannot reciprocate *your* surprise. I am merely what you have always seen—a country-bred girl, without fortune, or prospect of one, with a taste for playing the violin, and for speaking out my mind at any cost."

(Yes, there never was any one less at pains to be on the safe side than this young woman.)

"You are disgusted to find that I am not a poor relation," he ventured to remark.

"I am. You remember that on this very spot"—touching the railings with her fan—"two months ago, Colonel Sladen, with his usual delicate taste, joked pleasantly about the millionaire, your cousin. You laughed immoderately then. Yes, I remember, you actually shook the railings! And"—with increasing wrath—"you are smiling *now*. Of course it must be capital fun to take people in so successfully! to be able to laugh openly—as well as in your sleeve."

"Will you permit me to remind you of one small fact? Do you remember that you turned to me and said, that if I were *rich* you would never speak to me again? You were offering a premium on poverty."

"And I repeat that speech here," she said, once more turning to face him. "Now that I find you *are* rich"—she caught her breath—"I will never speak to you again."

"Oh, come, I say, Miss Gordon, you can't mean that," he expostulated. "At least you will give me a hearing. Be angry—but be just."

She made no reply, but began to strip little bits of bark from the rustic railing, to the utter destruction of her gloves.

"Admitted that I am the millionaire, that is merely to accept the nickname; for it is not I, but my uncle, who is wealthy. He made a fortune in trade, you know—Pollitt's pearl barley—and I am his adopted son. He has brought me up ever since I was ten years old, and has been awfully good to me."

Here she made an impatient movement, as much as to say, What was Mr. Pollitt's goodness to her?

He hurried on faster.

"I wanted to see something of the world. I was deadly sick of the routine of English life—hunting, balls, regattas, theatres; and I got my uncle's consent, with great difficulty, to spend a year in India. I was despatched with a valet, a cargo of kit, and the reputation of millions, with Waring as my guide, companion, and adviser. He is not related to me."

Honor looked at him with a half ironic smile, as much as to say, "Of course not! I should be surprised if he *were*."

"He is Mrs. Pollitt's brother; and she got him the berth, such as it was," pursued the young man doggedly.

"Little dreaming how luxurious it would become," added the young lady sarcastically.

"No, that was quite unpremeditated. When I first landed, I found that I had achieved a celebrity far beyond my wishes. I was supposed to be a Rothschild. I was bothered to death with touts and hawkers and all that sort of thing"—with a constrained laugh. "I saw that I'd have no peace till I got rid of all my extra luggage and the man. The combination branded me as 'valuable.' Waring had been in the country before, he knew the language and customs, so I made over my account at the bank into his name. He became paymaster, and we held our tongues—that was all. Waring looks rich, and has a genius for spending and making a splash. Now I have not. My tastes are inexpensive, and I have always told my uncle that nature intended me for a poor man."

Miss Gordon picked off another piece of bark with elaborate care, and then threw it away with an air of profound disgust.

"Our arrangement worked splendidly, as long as we were merely shooting and moving about; but when we came up here and began to know people, I saw that things were getting rather mixed—that it would not *do*, that we were carrying the idea too far. I spoke to Waring, and suggested taking the public into our confidence. He treated the matter as a joke, and asked if he should announce it in the *Pioneer*? I said, I thought that if he told it to one or two people as a dead secret, that it would be amply sufficient. But he would not hear of this, either in jest or earnest. He had, he acknowledged, played first fiddle too long to wish to change parts. He was most urgent that I should leave what he considered 'well' alone, and worked himself up into such a frightful state of mind—he put the whole thing so—so—so strongly—that I was obliged to leave matters *in statu quo*."

"Obliged!" echoed his fair listener, in a cool, incredulous tone.

"Yes, forced to do so." (He could not tell her of the reason which had been Waring's sole alternative.) "He said we had only a short time to put in, that it would make him look such an awful fool, that he had taken the reins to please me, and now I must sit tight to oblige *him*. In fact—to tell you a secret—that he would be in dreadful financial difficulties. All he wanted was *time*. If his creditors believed him to be a poor man, they would be down on him like a flock of kites. Two or three months would set him straight. So I yielded. But I made one stipulation; I said I must tell the truth to one person."

"And that highly honoured person?" she asked, with arched brows.

"Was yourself."

"Oh, monsieur, *c'en est trop*!" And she made him a deep inclination.

"Don't jeer at me, please," he exclaimed, in a low, sharp voice. "Once I was about to speak, and I was interrupted by the panther. Afterwards that intolerable child took the words out of my mouth, and you scorned them. For once in her life she told you the truth, the whole truth—I do love you."

There was no tremble or hesitation about these four syllables, but there was considerable amount of trembling about the hand which held a certain white feather fan, resting on the railings. The fan, unaccustomed to such uncertain treatment, slid swiftly away, and fell like a dead white bird into a lily bed below. No one sought it; seconds and sensations were priceless.

"I do love you, better than my own life; but I was afraid to speak, you were so down on money."

How could he guess at the nods, and becks, and wreathed smiles of certain busy old ladies near Hoyle, who had more than hinted at a speedy wedding and a rich husband, as the result of a trip to India? How could he know of blazing eyes and scarlet cheeks, and of a passionate repudiation of, if not India, at any rate a handsome future partner, and money?

"I meant to have told you to-night, on my honour I did; but with my usual cruel bad luck, that little beggar cut in before me. And you are dead against me, and with some reason, I confess; but you must not say that you will never speak to me again. Come, Miss Gordon, give me another chance." As she remained obdurately dumb, he continued with an air of quiet determination, "You will give me an answer by the time I have fetched your fan?"

Honor's anger had as usual cooled. She now began to see things from his point of view, and her indignation immediately transferred itself to Captain Waring. Mr. Jervis had been the tool and catspaw of that unscrupulous free-and-easy gentleman. Yes, she now understood the former's halting allusions to hunting and polo, his half-uttered sentences, and how he had suddenly paused, stammered, and would evidently have been glad to recall his own words. Once or twice she had caught a glimpse, instantly suppressed, of a slightly peremptory manner, the tone and air of one accustomed to being obeyed. She remembered, too, his easy familiarity with money, his—as she had hitherto considered it—insane generosity.

Meanwhile Mark ran down and picked up the white fan from its lily bed, shook the dew-drops from its delicate feathers, and, as he restored it to its owner, he looked straight into her eyes.

"Honor," he said, in a low eager voice, "you will let bygones be bygones, and forgive me, won't you?"

Honor hesitated, her lips trembled as if uncertain whether to laugh or to cry.

"You like me a little—I hope," he pleaded anxiously.

The lips broke into a faint but unmistakable smile.

"You are the only girl I have ever cared two straws about. I swear that this is the *truth*, and not the usual stock statement. I had a presentiment that you were my fate that night we walked along the railway line. That Eurasian fellow in the hut had a prophetic eye!"

"I am not so sure of that!" she said, with sudden vehemence. "You knew very well that you ought to have spoken out *long* ago."

"I would have spoken to you weeks ago, but that I was uncertain what answer you would give me."

"Oh!" recoiling with a gesture of indescribable horror. "What do you think I meant? I mean, that you might have let us all know who you were."

"Better late than never, I hope," he rejoined quickly. "My uncle knows all about you. May I speak to your aunt to-night?"

"What do you wish to tell her?" she faltered.

"That I am going to be her nephew," he answered, with the utmost composure.

"No—no—no," bursting into a half-hysterical laugh, "you must give me time—I want to think it over."

"Honor," coming close to her, and resolutely taking her trembling hand in his, "can you not think it over *now*? Will you marry me?"

Although her fingers shook in his hold, she held herself nervously erect, as she stood looking out over the moon-flooded mountains in silence, her eyes fixed on the far-away horizon with the gaze of one lost in meditation. She was crowding many thoughts into the space of seconds. Among them this—

"The gloved hand in which hers was imprisoned, how strong and steadfast—a brave hand to guide and support and defend her through life."

At last, with tremulous nervous abruptness, she made this totally irrelevant and unexpected remark—

"I wonder what people will say when they hear what a dreadful impostor you have been! Of course, I know what they will say of *me*—that I have guessed the truth all along—and have played my cards beautifully! Oh, I can hear them saying it!"

And she hastily withdrew her fingers, and looked at him with a mixture of defiance and dismay.

"You think more of what people will say than of me, Honor!" he exclaimed reproachfully.

"No, no!" filled with instant compunction, and her blushes as she spoke were visible even by moonlight. "I think more of you than of any one, Mark." Then, as if frightened at her own confession, she hastened to add, "Every one is going in, and here is my next partner coming to look for me."

"Let him look!" was the unprincipled answer. "Shall we go down and sit on the seat in the tennis-ground, by the big verbena tree?"

"But I am engaged to Major Lawrence," she objected, though she knew that resistance was useless.

"No doubt; but you are engaged to *me*—you and I are to be partners for life. Ah, ha!" with a triumphant laugh. "There, he has been waylaid by Mrs. Troutbeck—he won't get away from her under an hour. They are all going back," glancing at many other couples who were gravitating towards the club; "we shall have the place to ourselves. Come along," and leading her down the steps, they passed among glimmering flower-beds, and faint sweet flowers, to a recently vacated rustic bench. "I dare say you have often wondered what kept me at Shirani?" he began. "I came, in the first instance, hoping to meet my father. He has been thirty years out here, he was in the Indian Cavalry, and settled in this country, which he loves. My uncle is my adopted father, and I have seen very little of my real father since I was a kid; he lives in mysterious retirement in these hills, about fifty miles away, and is a widower for the second time. I have been waiting on week after week, hoping that he would send for me—that was my chief motive for remaining at Shirani. It is no longer so—as you very well know—in fact, of late, you have driven him clean out of my head!"

"If he were *my* father, I would go and visit him, without waiting for an invitation," said Honor, resolutely.

"I have written several times to say that I should like to see him, and asking when I might start—a plain enough hint, surely?"

"You are too punctilious. Why wait to be asked? There, that waltz is over; what a short one it was. Now I must really go in."

"What a thing it is to have a conscience! A strong sense of duty to one's partners!" he exclaimed with a laugh. "However, I am one of them myself, and I will let you off easily."

"No, thank you," she answered, with uncompromising rectitude. "Pray what about your own partners? And you are one of the hosts, too!"

"I see that I may always look to you now to remind me of my duty," he said, rising with extreme reluctance. "And I never felt more inclined to shirk it than now."

"I am sure I shall have quite enough to do to remember my own shortcomings; but at any rate I can manage to remind you of yours to-night. *We*," with a happy little sigh, "shall have to-morrow," and she also stood up to depart.

"Yes, please God, thousands of to-morrows. But, Honor, this one moment that you are so anxious to pass by and leave behind can never be repeated or effaced; this hour, when you gave yourself to me here, in this over-grown Indian garden, under the Southern Cross. When we are old Darby and Joan, sitting by our fireside in cold work-a-day England, we shall—at any rate, *I* shall—look back on this hour as sacred," and he put his arm round her and kissed her.

The intelligence that Jervis was the Simon Pure, the real, true, and only millionaire, was buzzed from ear to ear, and had soon spread over the club like wild-fire. Mrs. Brande ceased to yawn, fanned herself feverishly, and snappishly refused to believe "one single word of it." Mrs. Langrishe, for once, sat dumb and glum. More unlikely things had happened within her somewhat extensive experience. Colonel Sladen spluttered out his whole vocabulary of ejaculations and expletives, and Lalla Paske's eyebrows were almost lost to sight under her fringe! Of course it was the one and only topic; the air was still throbbing with the news, when, during a pause between two dances, Mr. Jervis and Miss Gordon walked into the ball-room. Their entrance produced quite a dramatic effect. How well-bred his air, how fine his profile and the pose of his head; with what easy grace his clothes sat upon him—clothes that were undeniably fashioned by a first-rate London tailor. These little details now struck people who had hitherto scarcely spared him a glance. As for Miss Gordon, she was always beautiful and charming. The pair made an uncommonly effective couple, and they looked so radiant, that their future happiness was evidently a settled thing. Yes, now that one came to think of it, they had *always* been good friends.

"And was it really thirty thousand a year? Was it in soap or pork? At any rate, it was a magnificent match for a penniless girl!" whispered a married lady to her partner.

"Of course the old woman was in the secret all along," remarked Mrs. Langrishe to a neighbour; "she is much cleverer than any of us have supposed. Oh, what a deep game she has played! *What* an old serpent!"

CHAPTER XXXI.
THE SUMMONS.

In the moonlight, bright as day, Mr. Jervis rode home beside Miss Gordon's rickshaw. Her tell-tale fan stuck out of the pocket of his overcoat.

Yes, their little world was not blind; it was evidently a settled thing. Most people were glad. The Brandes were sure to do the wedding in "style;" and a wedding would be an agreeable variety from dances and picnics.

"I shall come up to-morrow morning," he said, as he reluctantly released her hand, "to-morrow before twelve."

Mr. Brande, who had effected his escape early, had returned home, and been in bed and asleep for some hours.

He was suddenly aroused by his wife standing at his bedside, her cloak hanging off her shoulders, her coiffeur a little deranged, a lamp in her hand illuminating an unusually excited countenance.

"Well, *what* is it?" he demanded with pardonable irritation.

"Oh, P.! what do you think? A man has come from Simla——"

"Yes," suddenly sitting erect, his official mind at once on the alert for some pressing and important dispatch.

"He came out with them in the same ship," she panted.

Had Sarabella his wife gone suddenly out of her mind?

"He says that Mark, not Waring, is the rich man."

"He said it after supper, I suppose," snarled Mr. Brande. "He was *drunk*!"

"Not a bit of it! I tackled Mark himself, and he confessed. I was very angry at being taken in. He declares they did it without meaning a bit of harm at first, and that when it went too far he did not know what to do. He is very sorry."

"That he is a millionaire! Oh yes, I should think so!"

"He is coming up first thing to-morrow to tell you all about it; and, unless I'm mistaken, to speak to you about Honor."

"What about her?" sharply.

"Why, you dear, stupid man, are you asleep still? Can't you guess?"

"You told me that there was nothing of that sort; in fact," with an angry laugh, "that 'the boy,' as you called him, was desperately devoted to *you*."

"What stuff!" she ejaculated indignantly. "He will have thirty thousand a year! I know that I shall never close an eye to-night!"

"And are good-naturedly resolved that I am to keep you in countenance. You might, I think, have reserved this double-barrelled forty-pounder for the morning."

"And that's all the thanks I get," she grumbled, as she slowly trailed away to her dressing-room.

Just about this very time, Mark Jervis was smoking a cigarette in his bare sitting-room. Before him, on the table, lay a white feather fan and a programme. He was much too happy to go to bed, he wanted to sit up and think. His thoughts were the usual bright ones incident to love's young dream, and as he watched the smoke slowly curling up the air was full of castles. These beautiful buildings were somewhat rudely shattered by the entrance of his bearer—wrapped in a resai, and looking extremely sleepy—with a letter in his hand.

"A Pahari brought this for the sahib three hours ago," tendering a remarkably soiled, maltreated envelope.

Of course it was from his father at last. He tore it open, and this was what it said—

"MY DEAR SON,

"I am very ill. If you would see me alive, come. The messenger will guide you. I live forty miles out. Lose no time.

"Your affectionate father,
"H. JERVIS."

The letter was forty-eight hours old.

"Is the messenger here?" he asked eagerly.

"Yes, sahib."

"Then call up the grey pony syce; tell him to take gram and a jule, and saddle the pony. I am going off into the interior. I must start in twenty minutes."

The bearer blinked incredulously.

"I need not take you." The bearer's face expanded into a grin of intense relief. "I shall be away several days. Get out my riding kit, shove some clothes in a bag, and ask the cook to put up some bread and meat and things, and tell the coolie I will be ready very shortly."

Then he sat down, drew his writing-case towards him, and began to write a note to Honor. Her first love letter—and strange, but true, *his* also. It was merely a few lines to say he had been most suddenly called away by his father, and hoped that he would be back within the week.

It was both a keen disappointment and a keen pleasure to the girl when the ayah brought the letter to her at nine o'clock. She read it over and over again, but she will not allow our profane eyes to see it, nor can it be stolen, for she carries it about with her by day, and it rests under her pillow by night: at the end of the week it was getting a little frayed.

When the ayah handed the note to the Miss Sahib, the writer was already twenty miles out of Shirani, following a broad-shouldered Gurwali with his head and shoulders wrapped in the invariable brown blanket.

Their course was by mountain bridle-paths, and in an eastern direction; the scenery was exquisite, but its beauties were entirely lost upon Jervis, who was picturing other scenes in his mind's eye. The road crept along the sheer faces of bare precipices, or plunged suddenly into woody gorges, or ran along a flat valley, with cultivated fields and loosely built stone walls. The further they went, the lovelier grew the country, the wilder the surroundings. At twelve o'clock they halted to rest the grey pony—the messenger's muscular brown legs seemed capable of keeping up their long swinging trot all day. It was four o'clock in the afternoon when they arrived at their journey's end; they abruptly descended into a flat wooded dale, surrounded by hills on three sides, sloping away to the plains on the fourth. A path from the bridle-road led them into a dense jungle of high grass, full of cattle, pack ponies, and mules. Emerging from this, they came to a wall, along which they kept for about three hundred yards, and turning a sharp corner they found themselves outside a great square yellow house, two stories high.

It seemed as if it had been bodily transplanted from England. There was nothing irregular or picturesque about it—the windows were in rows, the roof was square and had a parapet, the sole innovation was a long verandah, which ran all round the building, and was apparently of recent date, a mere after-thought.

Mark, as he rode up to the steps, looked about him for the coolie; he had suddenly disappeared. There was no one to be seen. He ascended to the verandah, it was deserted, save for some fowl, who seemed delightfully at home. It was more the verandah of a native dwelling than the entrance to the home of an Englishman.

The new-comer gazed around expectantly, and saw three string charpoys, a bundle of dirty bedding, a pair of shoes, a huka, and a turban.

The door, which was innocent of paint or bells, was ajar. He pushed it open and found himself in a large, dim, very dirty hall. Here he was confronted by an old nanny goat, and two kids; to the left he saw a room, which appeared to be a mere repetition of the verandah.

As he hesitated and looked about, a man suddenly appeared, a servant presumably, wearing a huge red turban, and a comfortable blue cloth coat. He was stout and well to do, had a fat face, a black square beard, and remarkably thick lips.

He seemed considerably disconcerted, when he caught sight of the stranger, but drawing himself up pronounced the words, "Durwaza, Bund," with overwhelming dignity. Adding in English—

"The sahib never see no one."

"He will see me," said Mark, with decision.

"Sahib sick, sar, seeing no one, those my orders. Sahib seeing no sahibs for many years."

"Well, he sent for me, and I have come. Let me see him immediately. I am his son."

The Mahomedan's expression instantly changed from lofty condescension to the most unqualified astonishment.

"The sahib's—son!" he repeated incredulously.

"Yes. I have told you that once already. Look sharp, and send some one to see after my pony; I have come a long distance."

The bearer went away and remained absent about five minutes, during which time Mark had leisure to note the dirt, and neglected, almost ruinous, state of the house—which had originally been a fine mansion—to listen to loud jabbering and whispering in the room beside him, and to observe several pairs of native eyes eagerly peeping through a crack in the door.

"Come with me," said the bearer, with a sullen air. "The sahib will see you presently."

"Is he better?"

"Yes, he is quite well; please to sit here," and he opened the door of an immense dining-room, furnished with Bombay carved black wood furniture, and a dusty Indian carpet. It was a room that was evidently never used, and but rarely opened. Its three great long windows, which were caked and dim with grime, looked out upon the snows. This was evidently the back of the house; the front commanded a view of the plains. The site had been admirably selected.

A black tray, with cold meat and some very sour bad bread, was borne in, and a place cleared on the dusty table by the joint efforts of the sulky hearer and a khitmaghar, with a cast in his eye, and the very leanest figure Mark had ever beheld. However, he was much too hungry to be fastidious, and devoured the refreshments with a capital appetite. Meanwhile, after their custom, the two men stood by in silence with folded arms, staring with concentrated attention and unremitting gaze until the conclusion of the meal.

It was quite dark when the bearer reappeared, and, throwing open the door, announced in a deeply resentful tone—

"The sahib will see the sahib."

Mark followed the fat, square, aggressive-looking back, till he came to a curtained archway, and was ushered into a lofty dim room, so dim, that he could barely discern the figure which rose to greet him—a tall bent man in a dressing-gown.

"Mark, my boy, it was like you to come so soon," said a shaky voice. "Like what you were as a child," and he held out both his hands eagerly.

"I only got your letter at four o'clock this morning, sir," said his son. "I hope you are better?"

"I am for the present. I sent for you by a private messenger post-haste, because I believed that I had but a few hours to live, and I longed desperately to see you."

"I have been hoping you would send for me for the last two months. I have been waiting, as you know, in Shirani."

"Yes—yes—yes! Sometimes the temptation was almost irresistible, but I fought against it; for why should I cloud over your young life? However, I had no choice; the situation has been forced upon me—and you. My faithful companion, Osman, died ten days ago, but we will talk of this another time. These voices in my head interrupt me; especially that woman's voice," with an irritable gesture.

His son could not, for the life of him, think of any immediate or appropriate remark, and sat in embarrassed silence, and then Major Jervis continued—

"You are six and twenty now—a grown man, Mark, and speak like a man! I have not had a good look at your face yet. I wonder if it is the same face as that of my own honest-eyed boy?"

The answer would be prompt, if he so pleased, for the lean khitmaghar now staggered in under the weight of a large evil-smelling "argand" lamp (a pattern extinct everywhere save in remote parts of India).

Mark looked over eagerly at his father. His head was bent in his hands. Presently he raised it, and gazed at his son with a look of unmistakable apprehension. His son felt as if he were confronting an utter stranger; he would never have recognized this grey-haired cadaverous old man as the handsome stalwart sabreur he had parted with sixteen years previously. He looked seventy years of age. His features were sharpened as if by constant pain, his colour was ashen, his hands emaciated, his eyes sunken; he wore a camel's-hair dressing-gown, and a pair of shabby slippers.

"You are just what I expected," he exclaimed, after a long pause. "You have your mother's eyes; but you are a Jervis. Of course you see a great change in me?"

"Well, yes—rather," acquiesced his son, with reluctant truthfulness. "India ages people."

"You think this a strange life that I lead, I am sure; miles away from my fellow-countrymen, buried alive, and long forgotten?"

"No, not forgotten, sir. Do you recollect Pelham Brande of the Civil Service? He was asking for you only the other day."

"I think I remember him—a clever fellow, with a very pretty wife, who people said had been a servant. (How long these sort of things stick to people's memories.) I've been out of the world for years."

"But you will return to it. Come back to England with me. What is there to keep you in this country?"

"What, indeed!" with a jarring laugh. "No, my dear boy, I shall never leave the Pela Bungalow, as they call it, until I am carried out of it feet foremost."

"Why do you say this? You are a comparatively young man—not more than fifty-five."

"I feel a thousand years old; and I often wish that I was dead."

"I don't wonder! I should say the same, if I had lived here alone for seven years. How do you kill time?"

"I don't kill time. Time is killing me. I walk in the garden sometimes, but generally I sit and think. You must be tired, my boy," as if struck by a sudden thought.

"Well, I am, I must confess. I was at a ball until four o'clock this morning."

"A ball till four o'clock this morning!" he repeated. "How strange it sounds. It seems the echo of a voice speaking twenty years ago!"

Dinner was served at a small table; a fowl for Mark, some patent food for Major Jervis. The cooking was atrocious, the attendance careless, the appointments splendid, but grimy. It was the same in every department—an extraordinary mixture of squalor and magnificence. It seemed to the indignant young man that these ruffians of servants thought anything good enough for his father.

When Major Jervis's huka was brought in he looked over at his son and said—

"You smoke, of course?"

"Yes, thanks; but not that sort of thing. I would not know how to work it."

Last time he had lit a cigarette between four walls he little guessed at the style of his next surroundings. The room was not uncomfortable, the furniture was massively carved and luxurious, the carpet rich Persian; there were book-cases full of volumes, and there were fine pictures on the walls; but the paper was peeling off in strips, and cobwebs hung like ropes from the corners. The books were grimy with mould, the carpets and curtains inches deep in dust; certainly a sort of oasis had been cleared around Major Jervis's chair, but everywhere the eye turned were tokens of neglect, poverty, and decay. His father's slippers were in holes, his linen frayed; apparently he was a poor man. What had become of the begum's fortune?

CHAPTER XXXII.
"THE PELA KOTHI," OR "YELLOW HOUSE."

When Mark Jervis awoke the next morning, in a totally unfamiliar room, he wondered if he was dreaming, as he gazed at the heavy old carved furniture, the faded window hangings, the curious devotional pictures, and the little black crucifix and holy water receptacle at the foot of the bed. (The Cardozo family had of course been Catholics.) No, he was not dreaming, but actually under his father's roof at last.

As soon as he had dressed, he went out before breakfast to see after the welfare of his syce and pony. The yard resembled that of a serai, it was so full of natives, who gazed at him inquiringly, as he made his way through sheep, goats, buffalo calves, and children, to the stables, the tumble-down remains of what had once been an imposing pile. An old hairy Bhoetia pony and his own were now the sole occupants. His syce came to him eagerly, with a face of pitiful dismay.

"No gram for pony, sahib"—holding up his hands dramatically. "Never giving gram here—nothing."

"I'll see about that—go and buy some"—handing him rupees.

"Oh, sahib"—now putting his hands into an attitude of prayer. "Plenty, plenty Budmashes in this place. Sahib, let us travel to-day, quickly to Shirani."

"In a few days, Dum Sing—not yet; meanwhile take care of yourself and the pony." And he walked on to the garden.

The gardens, though somewhat neglected, were in perfect order in comparison to the house; they were laid out in stony terraces, the walls of which were loaded with fruit; there were flowers and vegetables in abundance, a round fish-pond, several statues, summer-houses, and a large staff of mallees working away with surprising zeal. A broad terrace walk commanded, as you arrived at one end, the snows, and a grand panorama of the plains as you reached the other. A well-worn track was beaten in the middle of this path, which indicated that it was a favourite promenade, and at the end nearest to the plains there was a seat.

Here Mark was joined by his father. He was dressed in a shrunken Puttoo suit, and looked frail and feeble, but such a gentleman in spite of all his shabbiness!

"This is my walk and my seat," he explained. "I sit here for hours. That white line far below is the cart road, and with a good glass you can make out carts and tongas; and far away on the plains, twice a day in clear weather, you can see the smoke of the train. So I get *some* glimpses of the world after all."

"And how are you off for neighbours, sir?"

"My nearest is an American missionary and doctor; he is twelve miles from here; and there is a German mission fifteen miles across that hill"—pointing with a stick.

"And your post? What about your letters?"

"Oh, I don't want a post; once in six months or so I send a coolie down to Ramghur."

"Then you don't take a daily paper?"

"Oh no; why should I? There are stacks of old ones about the house," was the amazing reply.

"And books?"

"I'm a man of one book. I read the Indian Army List; that is quite enough literature for me. Some fellow's names alone call up a whole novel."

"You feel better to-day, I hope?"

"Yes, I am unusually well. You are not married, are you?" he asked abruptly.

"No, not yet"—rather startled at the sudden change of topic. "But I hope to marry before long."

"Hope, hope; that's what we all say. Don't let it go beyond that. Hope told a flattering tale. I don't believe in hope."

"Why not?" inquired his companion rather anxiously.

"You see this terrace," he exclaimed, as if he had not heard; "I walk up and down it exactly a hundred times a day; I take a hundred beans in my pocket, and put one of them on that bench every time I come to it. I find it most interesting; only sometimes birds steal my beans, and that puts me out, and I lose count, and I have to begin the whole hundred over again, and I get so tired. But I must do it, or they would be angry."

"Who would be angry, sir?"

"I forget, just this minute—the beans or the birds."

"You seem to have wonderfully fine fruit-trees here," said Mark, after an expressively long silence.

"Yes, the mallees work well, the rascals, because I give them all the vegetables and flowers and fruit, as well as their wages. They make a good thing out of it; the peaches and pears and plums from the Yellow House are celebrated."

Mark now remembered having heard of their fame in far Shirani.

"Let us sit down here and talk," continued Major Jervis. "For once I will forego my walk; it is not every day that I have my son to listen to me. Recent events seem blurred and dim, but I remember years back distinctly. Mark, my boy, shall I tell you something about myself, and how I have spent my life? Would you care to know?"

"I would, of course."

"Then listen to me. You know I am the younger son of a good old family—Jervis of Jervis. My father, your grandfather, was General Vincent Jervis, and—I can't tell him *that*" (aside to himself). "My family bequeathed me a handsome profile, an aristocratic type of face, and something else (but I can't tell him *that*). I married for love, and I can recommend the experiment. Your mother and I scrambled along most happily, though I had always extravagant tastes—inherited, like my nose and yours. When she died, I lost my better half indeed—my headpiece, my best adviser, my all. I drifted back into my old squandering bachelor ways, and into debt; but I paid for you to the hour. Then I came across Miss Cardozo. She was not very young, but handsome, pleasant, and rich—she fell in love with me. I was a good-looking, dashing, devil-may-care major in a crack native cavalry regiment. She belonged to this country by race and taste. There was a good deal of the begum about her; she hated the idea of a stepson, and I reluctantly allowed your uncle to adopt you. I knew you would be rich and well cared for; but even then, I struggled against your uncle's persuasions. I must have had a presentiment of these days, when I would be desolate and alone. I was happy enough with Mércèdes; we led a gay, roving, extravagant life. We had plenty of friends, plenty of spirits, plenty of money. Mércèdes had no relations, but one, thank God; a greasy-looking cousin in Calcutta. Lord forgive me, but I hate him! My wife had a kind, warm heart, but she was passionate, excitable—and jealous. She allowed her feelings too much liberty; she slapped another woman's face at a public ball, she slippered her servants, she ran up huge bills, and she could never speak the truth. She actually preferred to tell a lie, even when she had nothing to gain by it. Can you imagine such a thing? However, we have all our faults; and she was a good soul, though she was not like your mother. They say a man prefers his first wife, a woman her second husband—what is your opinion, eh, Mark?"

"I am not in a position to offer one," he answered, with a smile.

"Oh, I forgot—of course not. Well, eight years ago this very month we were coming away from Mussouri to our place in the Doon; we were in the mail tonga, our ponies were half broken; though we had a good driver—the best on the road—it was all he could do to hold them, as they rattled down with the heavy steel bar, going clank, clank, clank. Just one mile out a goat on the cliff dropped suddenly into the road, the brutes shied wildly across, the strong wooden railings caught the side of the tonga, they strained—I hear them now—snapped, crashed, then there was a moment's mad struggle of driver and ponies—too late, over we went! They show the place still, I dare say—a drop of two hundred feet. The ponies were killed, and the driver and my wife. How I escaped was a marvel. My leg was broken, my head cut about, but I survived. Osman, my orderly, who had been in the old regiment for twenty years, nursed me, at Mussouri; and, as soon as I could be moved, I came here. I remembered it as a retired, quiet spot, with a charming garden. I wanted rest; my head was injured, and I thought I would pull myself together here, and then go home—but here I am still."

"Yes, but not for much longer," added his son, cheerily; "you will come home with me."

"Mércèdes' will was produced," he proceeded, calmly ignoring the question; "she had made it when she was not pleased with me, seemingly. This place and three hundred acres are mine, and one thousand rupees a month for life; also her jewels and gold ornaments—as much use to me as a heap of stones. Fernandez receives a fine income even now. All her wealth accumulates till my death, and then everything—jewels, rents, shares—goes to him. He is my heir. I cannot leave you a penny; nothing but the old Yellow House."

"I don't want the Cardozo money, sir."

"No; and you will have plenty. Meanwhile Fuzzil Houssan spends my income on his relations to the third and fourth generation, and laughs and grows fat."

"Surely you do not leave it all in his hands?" asked his listener incredulously.

"Yes, most of it. Only for that, I suppose he would poison me. I believe he is in Fernandez' pay—Fernandez, who I am keeping out of thousands a year. Occasionally he comes in person to see if there is any chance of my dying? I have given him great hopes more than once. Now that Osman is dead, he and Fuzzil will certainly hurry me out of the world—and that speedily."

"Who was Osman?"

"He was a sowar in my regiment—a Sikh—we had known each other for half a lifetime, and he was more to me than a brother. We joined the same month, we left the same day. He gave up home, country, people, and followed my fortunes, and died in my arms last week." Here Major Jervis's voice became almost inaudible.

"We had braved heat and snow, fire and water, together, and in the long evenings here whilst I smoked my pipe, he would talk to me by the hour of the old regiment; such talk is better than any book. If Osman had lived, I never would have summoned you—no, never; he stayed with me till death took him, and you must remain here till death takes *me*."

"*I* will take you with me," said his son, resolutely. "All you have been telling me shows me that this country is not the place for you. The sooner you are back in England, the better; you will come home with me, will you not?"

"I don't want to see England," he answered peevishly. "India is my country, it has got into my blood. I have spent my bright days out here, and here I'll spend my dark ones. My days are dark indeed, but they will soon be over, and so much the better. And now it is eleven o'clock," he said, rising stiffly. "Let us go in to breakfast."

After breakfast Major Jervis promptly disappeared, leaving his guest to wander about alone; to wonder at the extraordinary *ménage*, the troops of native children, pattering in and out, the fowl, the goats—who stumped through the hall as if they wore boots—the overpowering smell of huka, the great dreary rooms, piled up with rotting furniture, saddlery, and carpets. Among other wrecks, he noticed an old dandy and a side-saddle—doubtless the property of the dead Mércèdes.

He strolled about the valley, to the amazement of the hill people, who stared at him open-mouthed. How, he asked himself, was he to pass the long empty hours till sunset? For the bearer had condescendingly assured him, that "the sahib would sleep until then." He had taken a violent dislike to fat-cheeked Fuzzil, who scarcely troubled himself to obey an order, and had invariably to be summoned several times before he condescended to appear. A civil Pahari, touched by the young sahib's forlorn and aimless wanderings, volunteered to guide him to the cantonment. "A cantonment here?" he echoed incredulously, and accepted the offer with alacrity. A brisk walk by narrow tracks and goat-paths brought them to the brow of a hill in a southward direction, overlooking an abandoned station, Mark's guide volubly explaining to him that thirty years before had been full of gorrah-log (soldiers) from the plains. There were the barracks, the bungalows, and gardens, with trees that bore apples even now! But the cholera came one year and killed half a pultoon (regiment) and the rest went away, and never came back, except once or twice, so folks said, for "a tamashah."

"A tamashah—what do you mean?" asked Jervis, sharply. Was this burly hill man daring to chaff him?

"Sahibs and mem sahibs—eating, drinking, and having music and nautches. For the rest," with a shrug, "the place was given over to Bhoots and fiends."

A wide cart road, grass grown, led into the deserted cantonment, and Mark followed it on to the parade ground. There was the mess-house still habitable, the church roofless, encircled by a well-filled God's acre, kept in perfect order. Here was, indeed, a most surprising sight, a graveyard in the wilds, not over-grown or choked with weeds and bushes, but every stone and slab free from moss, every grave tended with reverent care. He went into the old echoing mess-house, and found it in excellent repair—thanks to its beams and doors of deodar wood—as the Pahari proudly pointed out. There were at least twenty bungalows standing, half buried among trees and jungle; with creepers matted down over their windows; in some the verandahs had given away, in some the roofs had fallen in, some, on the other hand, appeared to set time at defiance. The site was beautifully chosen, nestling in the lap of the hills, with a peep of the far-away plains; not a sound was to be heard save the trickling of a streamlet, nor a living thing to be seen, save a few hill cattle, and under a tree some vultures who were picking the bones of a dead pony. The condemned cantonment was, for all its beauty, a melancholy place. Beyond Haval Ghat, and sloping towards the plains, were fields of golden corn, and villages sheltering in clumps of trees, picturesque bananas waving their graceful leaves over huts, that with their comfortable slab roofs resembled English cottages.

The coolie now explained that he wished to show his honour yet another sight, and to guide him home by a different route.

Half an hour's climbing brought them to a good-sized street, of carved-fronted, flat-roofed hill houses. To the stranger's horror it seemed to be altogether populated by lepers—lepers who were old, middle-aged, young—there were also leper children. They swarmed out and surrounded the sahib, exhibiting every form of their hideous disease, as they clamoured for assistance. Jervis emptied his pockets of everything they contained in the shape of money, dispensed alms hastily, and among the worst cases, and then hurried away. He felt heartily ashamed of his feelings of shuddering repulsion. Supposing he had been a leper himself—and such things as Englishmen who were lepers were known to exist. Still he turned headlong from that awful village of life in death, and hastily reascended the hill towards the Pela Kothi.

The desolate cantonment and the leper-colony combined to depress him beyond words, although the scenery was unsurpassed, the air as exhilarating as a tonic, and the scents and sounds of the forest enough to stir the most torpid imagination; nevertheless, Mark Jervis felt as if he had a load upon his back, as if he had grown ten years older in the last two days. It was not merely the scenes of the afternoon that preyed on his spirits. There was his father—his mind was undoubtedly shaken—he must endeavour to get him away, to take him home; yes, at all costs.

"What a curious way he talked. Sometimes so well and sensibly; sometimes in such incomprehensible jargon. What did he mean by saying, 'Osman stayed here till death took him. You must remain here until death takes *me*'?"

CHAPTER XXXIII.
"HEREDITARY."

His long afternoon rest had revived Major Jervis; he appeared to be another man as he sat opposite his son at dinner, and talked not merely sensibly, but wittily, across the grimy tablecloth, on which was exhibited smoked goat-chops and other undesirable comestibles. He discussed the condemned cantonment—he recollected its bygone existence. The lepers—they were his pensioners, and came for their dole weekly—they were well looked after between missionaries and other people. He spoke of his regiment, his former comrades; he gave vivid descriptions of shikar expeditions, of pig-sticking, of thrilling scenes on active service. He related anecdotes of well-known people of his acquaintance; he boasted of his brothers-in-arms, and described a polo tournament as if it had come off yesterday!

"And you have quite lost sight of all these friends?" inquired his son, after a pause.

The question seemed to break a spell; all animation suddenly faded from the major's face, his whole expression changed into that of a shrunken old man as he replied—

"Yes; I left the herd, like a wounded deer, seven long years ago. I have hidden myself from them, and I am entirely forgotten. People are forgotten out here sooner, more completely, than in any other country."

"Why do you say so?" asked his son, incredulously.

"Because life is so full; events march rapidly, changes occur daily. Cholera, war, accidents, sweep away men—and memories."

When the table had been cleared and cigarettes produced, and Fuzzil and his satellite had somewhat reluctantly departed, Major Jervis looked steadily at his companion for some time, and exclaimed at last—

"You are very like me, Mark! I can see it myself; and I was considered a good-looking fellow. I had a bigger frame, though; I rode a couple of stone heavier. But you are a stronger man than your father; you have a square jaw and a stern will. You can say *no*. I never could get out that word in time—and many troubles were my lot. You wish me to go home with you, my boy?"

"I do," was the laconic and emphatic reply.

"And I want you to stay with *me*; you must remain with me. I have not long to live. Look at me well."

Mark glanced at his sunken eyes, his worn, emaciated features.

"And you must see the last of me. I don't intend to let you go; no, for once I, too, can say *no*."

"But, nevertheless, I'm afraid you must let me go, sir, and shortly. I promised Uncle Dan——"

"Yes," he interrupted with unexpected passion, "I understand what you would say; that you would thrust your uncle down my throat. But, after all, are you not *my* son—not his? I reared you until you were ten years old. When you were a small child and burning with fever, who was it that used to walk up and down with you in his arms for hours? Not your uncle Dan. Who was it that first set you on the back of a pony and taught you to sit like a Bengal sowar? Not your uncle Dan. Who was it that lifted you out of your dying mother's embrace? Not your uncle Dan. You are my own flesh and blood; in all the wide world I have now no one but you. Since Osman died I have not a single friend. I am surrounded by vampires of servants. My heir prays on his knees nightly to his patron saint for the telegram that will carry the news of my death. I believe the form is here in Fuzzil's possession, filled up, all but the *date*! I am a miserable, solitary, dying wretch, and I appeal to you, my son, to spare me a few months of your healthy, happy life, and to stay beside me and protect me. Do I," leaning his elbows on the table, and searching his son's face intently, "appeal in vain?"

"You wish me to live here with you altogether?"

"Yes," with curt emphasis.

"To give up my uncle?"

"For a time, yes. I seem cruelly selfish, but I am as a drowning man snatching at a spar. You *will* stay?" A tremor ran through his voice.

"I cannot. No; I promised Uncle Dan that I would certainly return," rejoined his son firmly.

"Your uncle has health, wealth, a wife, and many friends. Surely he can spare you to a sick and desolate man. The Almighty has afflicted me sorely. If you abandon me to my fate, and gallop back to your gay life and companions, the day will come when you will bitterly repent it. Osman's burthen has fallen on you, and will my own son do less for me than an alien in blood, a Mahomedan in faith, a poor, unenlightened, faithful sowar?"

And he stretched out his hand, and fixed an interrogative gaze on his companion. The paleness of concentrated feeling tinged the young man's face, a few drops of sweat stood on his forehead.

"Mark, what is your answer?" he demanded in a hoarse whisper. "Be quick. Say yes or no—yes or no."

"Not now, sir," suddenly standing up. "You must give me time. Give me forty-eight hours."

"Ah, there is something more than your uncle," with a swift expressive glance; and he rose and put his hands heavily on his son's shoulders. "I know," gazing straight into his eyes with a mad keenness in his look, "there is, of course, a *woman* in the case?"

"There is," admitted Mark, holding himself erect. "An hour before I got your letter, I had asked a girl to be my wife."

"And you need not tell me her answer—*yes*, of course; young, rich, handsome! The world is full of women—over-run with them. A man can have fifty sweethearts, but he has only one father!"

"There is only one sweetheart in the world for me," returned his son proudly.

Major Jervis drew himself up with an air of formidable dignity, and deliberately surveyed the speaker in sarcastic silence. Suddenly his expression changed, and became charged with fury; he made a frantic gesture, as if he would sweep both son and his sweetheart off the face of the earth. Then he tore back a purdah, beyond which he instantly disappeared—leaving it quivering behind him.

After waiting for a quarter of an hour, Mark went up to his own room, which he began to pace from end to end. Presently he turned down the lamp, flung open the window, looked out, and drew a long, long breath. His temples throbbed like engines in his burning head, every fibre of his being, every shred of his understanding, was now engaged in an inner soul-struggle.

On one side was arrayed Honor Gordon, his good-hearted, indulgent uncle, to whom he was sincerely attached—friends, wealth, the life to which he was accustomed—a life of ease and sunshine. On the other hand, there was *this*!—and he gravely surveyed the dim, weird landscape, the starlit sky, stretching to the mysterious horizon, and shuddered—his afflicted, forlorn father, who would not be removed, and who could not be abandoned.

His father, who had cared for him in his childhood. Yes! it was *his* turn now; and would he be behind Osman, the Mahomedan, who had done from love, what he should do from duty?

"But his father might live years! Was he a brute to wish him dead? *Did* he wish his father dead?" he asked himself fiercely, and shuddered again. What was he coming to? Had two days in the jungle turned him into a beast?

If he accepted what was plainly his duty, his uncle would cast him off, and he must renounce Honor Gordon! Was this a home to bring her to? common sense grimly demanded. And he would now be penniless indeed! He was tortured with heart-wearing doubts and temptations, as duty or inclination gained the upper hand. Two nights ago he could not sleep for happiness; now, he could not rest for misery! He resolved to walk down this raging fever, to quell this mental turmoil, by sheer bodily fatigue. He made his way through the silent house, where he found all the doors open, and nearly fell over a goat and two kids who were dozing in the hall, otherwise the lower regions were untenanted.

Suddenly he became aware of a great noise and brilliant light outside; laughing, loud chattering, and the complacent humming of dissipated tom-toms! The compound was illuminated by a large fire, and half a dozen flaming torches, and crowded with a mob of natives, who were enjoying, with intense appreciation, the solemn gyrations, and shrill high-pitched songs of a couple of tawdry Nautch girls. The surrounding go-downs were full of animated visitors. One was evidently a drinking den, whilst in another were gamblers. Standing in the shadow on the steps, unnoticed, Jervis surveyed these orgies entirely at his leisure. He distinguished the khitmatghar, though without a turban, his sleek black hair parted like a woman's, and falling over his shoulders. He was playing cards with three other men; a bottle and a beaker stood by for general enjoyment. The "khit" was absorbed in the game, his eyes seemed to protrude from his head as they greedily followed the cards. Meanwhile Fuzzil was solemnly superintending the Nautch, and applauding occasionally, with fitful, tipsy condescension.

A few sharp words from the young sahib, who appeared among them like a spirit, had an electrical effect. An awed and immediate silence was followed by a simultaneous helter-skelter rush and scurry.

"What is the meaning of this madness?" demanded the sahib sternly of Fuzzil, who with drunken valour stood his ground, whilst the Nautch girls, tom-toms, and spectators, melted away like so many rabbits scuttling to their burrows.

"Madness!" repeated Fuzzil, with an air of outraged dignity; "it is a grand tamasha for the marriage of my wife's brother's son. Does the sahib not like Nautches, and cards, and drink, like other young sahibs? Of a surety he *does*"—answering his own question with insolent emphasis, and a little stagger. "As for madness; this house is a poggle-khana" (madhouse).

"What do you mean, you rascal?" said Jervis, sharply.

"Of a truth, all the world know that. Is the fair-haired sahib, his son, the *last* to learn that the old man is mad? Ask the doctor; ask Cardozo Sahib. Sometimes for one year he never speaks. Sometimes bobbery and trying to kill himself; but Osman took care of him. Now, lo! Osman is dead; there will be an *end* soon. This house will cease to be a poggle-khana, and all the worthy 'nouker log' (servants) can return to their own country."

"You, for one, can return to-morrow," responded the sahib, in surprisingly fluent Hindostani.

"You are not the master here," blustered Fuzzil, in amazement. "I taking no orders."

"You will find that I am; and if you ever again come into my presence, with your shoes on your feet, I will thrash you within an inch of your life. Send away all these people; tell them the tamasha is over for to-night; put out the lights, and get to your go-down, and sleep yourself sober."

Fuzzil stared, swallowed, gasped. The young man's resolute air and stern eye were altogether too much for him, and he obediently slunk off, without further dispute.

Major Jervis did not appear the next morning, and his son mounted his pony and went for a long ride. Where he went he but vaguely remembered; his thoughts were far too preoccupied to note his surroundings. There was no doubt that his father's mind was affected; no doubt this was attributable to the fall over the khud, and injury to his head. The vital question remained to be decided, was he, Mark Jervis, to sacrifice his youth to filial duty?—one would soon grow old in the Yellow Kothi—to renounce friends, fortune, sweetheart, to lead a semi-savage existence, entirely cut off from what is called Life.

But, on the other hand, if he set his pony's head for Shirani, and returned to Honor, to all the delights of the world, would not the recollection of the miserable father he had abandoned to strangers poison every pleasure, and force itself into every joy?

"But to live there"—and he drew rein and gazed down upon the square house, standing out distinctly against a blue, purplish background—"will be," he exclaimed aloud, "a living death. Like a vain young fool, I wanted a chance to do something—some special task, some heroic deed, that would set me apart from other men; but, God knows, I never thought of *this*!"

It was late in the afternoon when he rode up to the verandah, and was amazed to meet a coolie leading away a steaming-hot hill pony—a hired animal—and more surprised still to discover a visitor comfortably established in a long chair, with his fat legs elevated above his head, enjoying a peg and a cheroot. Evidently there was no occasion to ask him to make himself at home! The stranger slowly put down his feet and stood on them, when he first caught sight of Mark.

After staring hard for a few seconds, he said, with an air of great affability, "I am Fernandez Cardozo, and you are Major Jervis's son—my cousin."

"I am Major Jervis's son," assented the young man, stiffly; and he, in turn, critically surveyed his father's heir. He was low-sized, fleshy, and swarthy, about forty years of age; he had a closely cropped bullet head, sprinkled with grey hairs, a round good-natured face, a pair of merry black eyes, and a large mouthful of flashing white teeth. An Eurasian, and possibly not a bad sort of fellow, was Mark's verdict.

The other was thinking, "What a fine young man! Quite tip-top. How strange it seemed that he should be the son of the poor, crazy old major inside." And his eyes travelled over his smart country-bred pony, his English saddlery, his well-cut boots and clothes.

"Yes—you are his son," he said at last, "but I am his *heir*. We are, son and heir," and he laughed—an oily laugh.

"You are heir of course to Mrs. Cardozo—I mean Mrs. Jervis's fortune. Won't you sit down?"

"You have not been long here, have you?" now reseating himself.

"No; only two or three days."

"And how," with a jerk of his thumb in the direction of the major's apartments, "do you find the old man?"

"Well, I never knew until now, that his mind was rather—affected. He has not written to me for years, and I only got his address with difficulty."

"Yes, he prefers to lie low—as Mr. Jones. But '*rather* affected,' is putting it mildly."

"Do you think so?" considering Cardozo with a pair of hostile eyes.

"You will think so too before long. Now don't be vexed with me, my dear boy. No one is ever angry with Ferdy Cardozo, they know I am a good fellow, and that I mean well. Shall we go inside and see if there is anything to be had to eat?"

"Certainly, I ought to have thought of it before."

"Oh, please don't apologize, I'm quite at home. Fuzzil, you fat lazy swine," to the now obsequious bearer, "get me something to eat, none of your dogs' food—such as brain cutlets or Irish stew, and bring up some of *my* wine. It's very hot in here, awfully frousty," opening a window. "The major hates me like poison, and when he hears I'm in the house he won't come out, he will go to ground like a snake, but I shall be off to-morrow."

"Yes?" interrogatively.

"Are you in the army?" continued Fernandez with half-closed eyes.

"No, I am not in the regular army; I'm in the yeomanry."

"No profession then?" raising his arched brows in rather supercilious surprise.

"No, not any." His profession as heir to his Uncle Dan, would soon be a thing of the past.

Mr. Cardozo's surmise was perfectly correct. Major Jervis did not appear, he merely sent his salaams and dined in his own apartments, leaving his son and his heir to consume that meal *tête-à-tête*. It was a great improvement on the usual *menu*. Evidently Fuzzil had resources that he drew upon on worthy occasions.

"It's a fine moonlight night," remarked Fernandez. "Let us go and smoke in front of the house, it's better than being indoors, and I like to make the most of the hill air when I'm up, and we are out of the way of eavesdroppers."

In a few moments they were sitting on the low wall in front of the Pela Kothi.

"Osman was a desperate loss," began Fernandez as he struck a fuzee—"a desperate loss."

"So I gather from what I hear," assented his companion.

"That's partly what brought me up. I have business round here, of course, though. I live in Calcutta. I like to keep my eye on the property, and I look after the major and manage his affairs as well as I can—I feel it my duty." And he began to smoke.

Was here yet another man, of no kin to Major Jervis, who was to put his own flesh and blood to shame?

"I wish you would tell me something about my father—the last seven years are a sealed page to me."

"Well, first of all he got a fall on his head pig-sticking, and that made him rather foggy for a bit, he saw everything double. Then of course the tonga business was a finisher. Osman brought him here, and at times he was perfectly well, as sane as you or I, and interested in the garden, and the news, and all that, but he got worse by degrees, fits of silence and depression, never opening his lips for maybe a whole year—melancholy, suicidal mania—tried to hang himself with a stirrup leather, you understand," lowering his voice expressly.

"*I*—I—understand," acquiesced the other, almost in a whisper.

"He must have some one always with him, more or less. Some one whom he likes, and who has influence and a strong will, such as Osman—he was invaluable. I don't know how we are to find a substitute for him," continued Fernandez thoughtfully, as he crossed his legs, leant his elbow on his knees, and puffed meditatively.

"The servants he has about him now must be shunted," said Mark, emphatically. "I never saw such a pack! They had a feast and tom-toms last night. They are lazy, insolent, useless blackguards!"

"Not a doubt of it," agreed Fernandez, cheerfully. "And Fuzzil will retire a rich man, keep a gharry, and send his sons to college. They come here fairly decent servants—but the desperately dull life, no bazaar, no other 'nauker log' to bukh with, is a want no wages can repay. Then the household has no head, no regular hours, and so they all do as they please and go to the bad. I don't know what is to be done now—your father won't allow a stranger near him. The question is, Who is to replace Osman? Tell me that"—and he flung out his hand with a dramatic gesture.

"I will replace Osman," was the totally unexpected reply.

"You!" cried Cardozo, gazing at the speaker with round-eyed incredulity. The young man's face was pallid, his lips set hard. "You don't know what you are saying"—and he took his cheroot out of his mouth and continued to stare at his companion exhaustively. "You are accustomed to the big world of London; you have seen and done what I have only read about—for I have never been home; you are accustomed to a whirl of society, to novelty, excitement, luxuries, and immense wealth. *You* to live here? Upon my word, excuse me, my dear fellow, the very *idea* makes me laugh. Even I, born and bred in the country, would go mad in a very short time. I could not stand the life for more than a week—a month would kill me!"

"I am not so easily killed as you imagine. I am tougher than you think," rejoined Jervis.

"But you do not know what you would have to endure"—throwing out his arms excitedly. "The solitude, the silence, day after day, exactly the same—breakfast, tiffin, dinner, bed—nothing to do, nothing to hope for, no one to see, except the hill-folk or a missionary. I tell you that you would do one of two things—either cut your throat, or take to drink."

"Your eloquence is a loss to the bar, Cardozo."

"So I have often been told"—with a hasty movement of his hand; "but it is not a question now of my eloquence, but of your future. Do you generally mean what you say? Do you intend to live here as your father's sole companion?"

"I do," replied the young man, answering his look with eyes full of indomitable fire.

Mr. Cardozo puffed away in solemn silence for some time, but there was a certain brisk cheerfulness in his air as he suddenly remarked—

"The major is going downhill rapidly, poor old chap! His health is bad; I see a great change in him. His mind will never recover. Of course *that* is not to be expected; you know that it runs in the family—it is hereditary."

"What runs in the family? What is hereditary?" demanded the other, with a look full of pain and excitement.

"Insanity. He told Mércèdes, who told me, that his brother jumped overboard at sea, going home in charge of two keepers; and his father died in Richmond lunatic asylum."

"Is—this—true?" Mark brought out the words in three quick gasps.

"You don't mean to say that you never knew? Oh, I'm awfully vexed! I entirely forgot you were his son. You look so different, upon my word, as you stand there, that I cannot realize that he is anything to you."

Jervis struggled to articulate again, but signally failed. With a shaking hand he tossed his cigarette over the parapet, and then walked away up the steps, and was instantly merged in the gloom of the entrance.

"Hereditary." The word seemed written before him in letters of flame—"hereditary."

CHAPTER XXXIV.
THE INITIALS "H. G."

When it became known at the club, and subsequently all over Shirani, that young Jervis had suddenly disappeared the night of the bachelors' ball, great was the sensation.

No, no, there was no suspicion of foul play; there were his servants to be questioned. Jan Mahomed, his respectable, grey-bearded attendant, had declared that the night his master had come home, he had got straight from his evening clothes into his riding things, and had taken the grey pony and galloped away into the darkness. Whither? How could he say? holding out a pair of lean, empty hands, with a gesture of pitiable ignorance. He made no mention of the letter; for this prudent retainer had lived with bachelor sahibs before.

Mrs. Langrishe and Lalla were for once agreed. They were convinced that Mr. Jervis had gone further than he had intended with Miss Gordon, and to repair the error, had subsequently put miles between them—was probably by this time on blue water. But they did not venture to air this opinion openly; it was reserved for "ladies only." Major Langrishe had laughed it to scorn; and as for Toby Joy, he and Lalla almost had a quarrel on the subject—their very first quarrel.

"Jervis to propose to a girl, and then run away!" he cried indignantly. "About the last fellow in Shirani to do such a mean trick. Jervis is a gentleman to the soles of his boots, and a real good chap, worth fifty of Waring."

"Yes, so we all learn *now*, when it's rather late in the day," retorted Lalla, sarcastically.

"You mean about the money! But I mean in other ways. He took it awfully well the day I nearly smashed up him and Mrs. Sladen; you saw that yourself! He certainly lay low with regard to the fact of his being wealthy. He is the least ostentatious fellow I ever met, and as straight as a die, a complete contrast to the great Clarence, who has been playing the deuce up at Simla, by all accounts, and making ducks and drakes of any quantity of coin."

"Well, at least, we know *where* he is, and *what* he is doing!" retorted Lalla. "But no one can say the same of the cousin. Where is he, and what is *he* doing? He was always very close about himself, and I consider the whole thing most suspicious. Supposing a man proposed for me."

"Yes, supposing a man proposed for you," repeated Toby, edging nearer to the lady.

"And I accepted him. Now, don't look so utterly idiotic, for mercy's sake! And he simply took to his heels and ran away, would I not think that peculiar conduct? I must say Honor Gordon takes it better than I should, under the circumstances."

"How soon are you going to get rid of that fellow Gloster?" inquired Toby irrelevantly.

Sir Gloster was bringing a tedious convalescence to an end, and taking daily airings in Mrs. Langrishe's rickshaw; and people, who were disappointed of a wedding in one quarter, were eagerly expecting to hear of one in another.

"I don't know," coquettishly. "Perhaps I may *never* get rid of him!"

"You know you only say that to make me wretched. You don't really mean it, do you?" pleaded Toby, with such a look of misery on his usually merry face, that Miss Paske burst into an uncontrollable scream of laughter, and said—

"Toby, how can you be so exquisitely silly?"

The few days Mark Jervis had written of had grown into ten, and he had almost slipped out of people's minds, save when a string of ponies being led along by their syces, and wearing smart jhools, with the initials M. J., brought him momentarily to remembrance.

And now Captain Waring suddenly reappeared. He came direct from Simla, back to despised Shirani, and in anything but his usual cheery spirits. How he had cursed his coolies and ponies on the way up! What a life the *débonnaire* Clarence had led his miserable servants, as if the poor wretches were responsible for his discomfiture, his bad luck, his ruin, for it had come to that—and it was a desperate man, who spurred his distressed country-bred pony up the last two miles of the dusty cart road.

He was surprised to find Haddon Hall tenantless; but when the bearer explained how "a Pahari had brought a note, and his master had gone 'ek dum,'" *i.e.* on the spot, he nodded his head sagaciously, and appeared to understand all about it. What he could not comprehend was Mark's prolonged absence. "Ten days gone," Mahomed said; "two days, were he in Mark's shoes, would be amply sufficient time to devote to his eccentric parent."

Clarence was in a bad plight, and almost at the end of his resources, which had hitherto been as unfailing as the widow's cruse. He had gambled recklessly, with stronger men than himself; he had thrown good money after bad, in the usual wild attempt to recover both. His I.O.U.'s and debts of honour and lottery accounts came to a large total; he would be posted in a few days if he did not pay up. As to other debts, they were legion—shop bills, club and mess accounts, wages—they poured down on him in all directions, ever since that little brute Binks had peached at Simla and spoiled everything. Miss Potter had bitterly upbraided him, and subsequently snubbed him unmistakably; the men at the club looked coldly on him; the high players in the card-room had seemed stiff and curiously averse to his "cutting in." People suddenly stopped talking when he joined them; yes, he was at a crisis in his life, a crisis brought on by his own insane recklessness, and raging passion for play. He had come expressly to Shirani to get Mark to assist him; if he failed him, if he refused to stretch out a hand, and drag him back from the gulf of insolvency and disgrace, on the brink of which he tottered, down he must go, and be swept away and swallowed up, among the thousands and thousands who have similarly gone under!

After a bath, a meal, and a smoke, Captain Waring felt better, and set to work to think things out steadily, and to pull himself together. He had sold his own ponies and guns, their price was a sop to his most urgent creditors. He would now proceed to dispose of Mark's battery. Yes, they were fine weapons—he would put them and the ponies on the notice board at the club at once—the price of them would pay their passages and immediate expenses; Mark's £500 would cover all debts; he had not a rupee left at the agent's, and he would make Mark come home at once. It was true that their year's leave had yet four months to run, this was the middle of June, but he had made India too hot to hold him for the second time. The sooner he set about winding up affairs the better, and he rose on the spur of the moment, resolved to cast an eye over his cousin's saleable effects.

He went into Jervis's room, the smaller and worst of the bedrooms, and very plainly furnished. There was a bare camp bed, a rickety chest of drawers, a washed-out dhurrie on the floor, also a long row of boots; a couple of saddles on a stand, and a first-rate battery of guns—"a double-barrel central-fire breach-loader, by Purdy, that will fetch 250 rupees; a 500 express, by Lancaster, 400 rupees; 8-bore rifle, 600 rupees; rook rifle, 100—say, 1300 rupees," was his mental calculation.

When he had examined these, a parcel on the chest of drawers arrested his attention; there was also a programme. He took it up and looked it over; he was extremely inquisitive in such small matters. The card was full, and opposite three dances were scribbled the initials "H. G."

"Humph!" he muttered aloud. "So *that* is going on!" And as his gaze travelled to a ladylike parcel in silver paper—"What the dickens is *this*?"

He promptly unrolled it, and beheld a most superior white ostrich feather-fan, with the monogram H. G. on the handle. Captain Waring unfurled it, fanned himself slowly, folded it up once more, and said—

"A feather shows how the wind blows, Mark my boy! Well, I'll go over to the club and hear what is going on, look up the mail steamers, and offer your ponies and rifles, my fine fellow. You will have to come home with me sooner than you think, and I'll get great kudos from the uncle for carrying you off from a dangerous entanglement—in other words, from H. G."

And Captain Waring sauntered out to the stables in a surprisingly good humour.

"I'm sorry he has got the grey with him!" he muttered to himself; "the grey is a long way the best of the three! The grey is worth five hundred rupees."

Strange to say, the grey, carrying his owner, arrived home that same day about four o'clock, much to the bearer's joy. His master spent the afternoon packing, making arrangements, giving orders, writing letters. He announced that he was going away again the next morning, and Jan Mahomed and his son were to follow with all his baggage. In future he would live with his father near Ramghur.

Jan Mahomed received this astounding piece of information in the usual native fashion, merely with a stolid face and a long salaam.

Yes, his choice was made, the die cast, to Major Jervis's intense satisfaction, and to Fernandez Cardozo's intense amazement. The former had been ill, and had detained his son from an earlier return to Haddon Hall to wind up his affairs, and open his letters, the latter including one from his uncle, which had been lying on the writing-table for a whole week. It said—

"DEAR MARK,

"Yours received, and I answer it within the *hour.* I note all you say about the young lady, and I don't like the idea *at all.* My boy, you know I have never refused you anything, but I must say *no* to this. I have only your welfare at heart. I cannot allow you to throw yourself away on an ordinary Indian spin. You are right to tell me all about it; and, as you have not yet proposed for her, *don't.* You must marry some pretty, well-born girl, who has never been through the Suez Canal. Come home immediately; these idle days in a hill station have had a bad effect on your steady brain. Come home as soon as ever you can. Your father has evidently become naturalized; he does not want you—*I do.* As for the girl, you might give her a pony, or a diamond brooch—anything—everything, but yourself.

"Your affectionate uncle,
"D. POLLITT."

As Mark looked up from this letter he met the scrutinizing black eyes of Jan Mahomed which were fixed upon his face.

"This sahib has been ill," he said, severely. "Jungle fever getting?"

"No, Jan, I am all right. This is the day the English dak goes out, and I want you to take a letter to the post for me, it will be ready in twenty minutes, and send word to the Captain Sahib, that I have come back."

Then he drew his writing-case towards him and began a letter to his uncle. Evidently this letter was not an easy composition, in fact, he had already written it several times at Ramghur, and then instantly destroyed it, but it must be written somehow, and *now*. The post left within the hour. At length he wrote—

"DEAR UNCLE DAN,

"Since I last wrote to you I have been with my father; he sent for me suddenly, and I went off the same hour, as his note said that he was very ill. I found him living forty miles from this, in an isolated house, part of the Cardozo property, and under the name of Mr. Jones—a name he has adopted for the last seven years. I never would have recognized him, he is so broken down, and quite an infirm old man. This is the effect of the accident that killed his wife. But this is not the worst. His mind is deranged, which accounts for his strange silence and many other things. At times, such as at the present moment, he is perfectly clear and collected, but at others he suffers from depression and melancholia, and sits silent for days and weeks. He is alive to his own infirmity, and that is why he has chosen this life of seclusion. Until recently he had one of his former sowars living with him, an invaluable companion; and now that he is dead—an irreparable loss—Uncle Dan, I am going to tell you something that will be a shock, as well as displeasing, to you—I am about to take the place of this faithful servant, and endeavour to be his substitute. My father is a forlorn and stricken man; he has no one but me to look to—he does look to me, and I will not fail him. He is not wealthy—the begum's riches, Mrs. Jervis's fortune (minus a certain annuity), is strictly reserved for her next of kin, Fernandez Cardozo. He is not a bad sort, and has been looking after my father and his affairs—in short, fulfilling *my* duty; but I shall relieve him of all this, and remain out here as long as my father lives. I am afraid that at first you will think I am treating you badly and ungratefully; but this I know, that, were *you* in my place, you would do the same yourself. Of course I forfeit all claim on you by such a step as I am about to take, and it is a step which has cost a struggle. I am going to lead a different life to that to which I have been brought up. I shall be isolated and out of the world, for I can never leave my father even for a day. Once I take up my post, I shall stick to it.

"I have found your letter here awaiting me—your letter about Miss Gordon. Of course that is all at an end now. As for her not being good enough for me, it is the other way about. She is the only girl I ever cared for. I shall never marry now, but will adopt the profession I chose as a child, and live and die a bachelor. I wonder that I can joke, for I need hardly tell you that I am not in a merry mood. I feel as if everything had gone from me at one blow, and I am left face to face with a new life and an inflexible duty. Whatever you may think of me, Uncle Dan, my feelings towards you will never change; I shall always think of you with affection and gratitude.

"Clarence came back to-day from Simla. I have not seen him as yet. I only arrived a couple of hours ago, to collect my kit, dismiss my servants, and say good-bye to Miss Gordon. If you had ever seen her, and spoken to her, you would not have written that suggestion about a pony or a brooch. I go back to Ramghur to-morrow. My lot is not likely to be a very bright one; do not make it harder, Uncle Dan, by being implacable. I know that at first you will feel certain that you never *can* forgive me, but you will by-and-by. Write to me and send me papers to care of Mr. Jones, Ramghur, *viâ* Shirani. You may as well take my name off the clubs, sell the horses down at the farm, and tell Windover not to put the drag in hand.

"Your affectionate nephew,
"M. JERVIS."

This letter, hastily written, with numerous erasures, the writer did not trust himself to read over, but thrust it into an envelope, addressed and despatched it on the spot, as if he almost feared that he might be tempted to recall it, and change his mind.

CHAPTER XXXV.
"OSMAN'S SUBSTITUTE."

"Hullo, Mark!" cried his travelling companion, with cordial, outstretched hands. "So you are back? I only arrived this morning—came straight through from Simla. What's the matter, eh? You seem rather choop."

"Oh, I'll tell you presently. Let us have your news first."

"On the principle of keeping the best for the last, eh? for mine is *bad.* Well, as for news"—removing his cap and sitting down—"I suppose you have heard that our secret is now public property. That blatant ass, little Binks, had it all over Simla. What business had *he* to thrust himself into our private affairs?"

"It was never what you would call private," rejoined Mark, who was leaning against the end of a real old-fashioned hill sofa, with his hands in his pockets. "I am only surprised that it never came out before."

"Yes, now that you mention it, so am I. We had a good many fellow-passengers, but they none of them came up this way; they were mostly for Burmah, or Madras, or globe-trotters. I could not give the name of one of them if I got a thousand pounds. There is nothing one forgets so soon as a fellow-passenger. Of course you have been to see your governor?"

"Yes. I've been away nearly a fortnight."

"And how did you find him?"

"I am sorry to say very broken down—ill and desolate."

"But with sacks of gold mohurs all round the rooms, and chandeliers of real diamonds. I hope you have some in your pockets?" said Waring, gaily.

"No. He is a comparatively poor man; at least he has just enough to live upon—an annuity. The bulk of his fortune goes, as it ought to go, to the Cardozo family."

"Well, one fortune is enough for you," rejoined Clarence. "I came up post haste. I rode your bay pony in the last ten miles, and, by Jove! I thought I had killed him. It was frightfully hot, and I put on the pace. I gave him a whole bottle of whisky when I got in."

"A whole bottle! Well, I hope you will give him some soda-water to-morrow morning. What a head the poor brute will have!" he added, with a wintry smile. "But what was the reason for such desperate riding? Has Miss Potter come back?"

"Miss Potter be hanged!" was the unchivalrous reply. "I came up as hard as I could lay leg to the ground to get you to help me out of an awful hole—an infernal money muddle."

"To help you again! I thought that five hundred pounds would put you straight."

"Good heavens, man! it's not hundreds, but thousands that would do that!" cried the prodigal.

Jervis ceased to lounge, and now assumed a more uncompromising attitude.

"Explain," he said laconically.

"Yes; I've been going it, my boy," admitted Waring, with a reckless laugh. "Old faces, old places, were too much for me, and I dropped a pot of money. There was a fellow from New Orleans, a long-headed chap, a born gambler, and a wild-looking Hungarian count; they carried too many guns for me. One night we had three thousand pounds on the turn of a card. Ah, that is living! There is excitement, if you like! Better twenty hours of Simla than a cycle of Shirani."

"Nevertheless you have returned to Shirani?"

"Yes, only because I am cleared out," was the absolutely unabashed reply.

"I'm sorry to hear it, Clarence; but it is not in my power to help you beyond the five hundred pounds that will pay our expenses here. The table was papered with bills when I came back."

"Oh, those!" with a gesture of scorn, "rubbishy little shoeing accounts, stable accounts, and rent. I don't mind *them*, it's others. I'm really in an awful hat this time and no mistake, and you must assist me."

"I cannot."

"I tell you again that you must!" cried Waring, throwing himself back in his chair, with an energy that made that venerable piece of furniture creak most piteously.

"There is no 'must' in the matter," retorted the other steadily, "and if I were in the humour for joking—which I am not—the comic side of the situation would make me laugh. You were sent out by Uncle Dan as my mentor, to keep me straight, to give me the benefit of your experience and to show me round. Wasn't that the arrangement? But, by Jove," suddenly springing up and beginning to pace the room, "I have been lugging you out of scrapes ever since we landed in the country!"

"It is a true bill, oh wise, cool-headed, and most virtuous Saint Mark! This, I most solemnly swear to you, is my last and worst scrape. Get me a cheque for a certain sum, wire to the uncle to lodge it at the agents, and I'll be a truly reformed character, and never touch another card, for ever and ever, amen."

"And afterwards?"

"Afterwards we will reward the old man, and rejoice his heart, by packing up and going home by the next steamer. He would give many thousand pounds to get you back again—you are the apple of his little pig's eye. This country does not agree with me—I don't mean physically, but morally. It's an enervating, corrupting, beguiling land. We will sell off your guns and ponies, dear boy. I've put them up at the club—I hope I have not broken the wind of that dark bay—we will go down in the mail tonga this day week, *en route* for Bombay. There are temptations for *you* in this Indian Empire too. The sooner you say good-bye to H. G. the better. Now, there is my programme for you—my new leaf. What have you to say to it?"

Brisk and confident as his speech had been, there was a certain unmistakable lameness in its conclusion. Waring had secretly winced under his listener's eyes—his listener, who sat motionless, contemplating him with an expression of cool contempt.

"The first thing I have to say is, that my guns and the ponies are not for sale, or only the chestnut with the white legs."

"Great Scot! You don't mean to tell me that you intend to take three ponies home! And what do you want with an express rifle and an elephant gun in England?"

"I may require them out here. I am not going back to England."

Captain Waring sat suddenly erect.

"Of course this is all humbug and rot!" he exclaimed vehemently.

"No. I am quite in earnest. I intend to remain with my father; it is the right thing for me to do. He is alone in the world; his mind is weak."

"So is his son's, I should say," burst out Waring, throwing his cigarette into the verandah. "Get him a keeper—two keepers, by all means; a baby house, a barrel organ, every comfort, but don't *you* be a lunatic. Come home with me. Think of Uncle Dan!"

"Yes, I know very well that Uncle Dan will cast me off; he told me he would, if I remained out here with my father."

"Cast you off!" almost screamed the other. "Do you mean to tell me that you will never see the colour of his money again?"

"Never."

"I believe that Miss Gordon has something to say to this scheme, as well as this mad Quixotic idea about your father," cried Clarence, crimson with excitement. "As for the girl, you must let her slide, we have all been through *that*; but, for God's sake, hang on to the uncle, and the coin. You are the only mortal for whom he will open his purse-strings."

"I have written to him, and told him that I am not going home."

"Is the letter posted?"

Mark nodded.

"Then," turning on him fiercely, "you have burnt your boats."

"I have."

"You are mad to chuck everything at twenty-six years of age. You give up your life at home——"

"I know best what I am giving up," interrupted his companion impatiently. "I know that I am going back to Hawal Ghât to-morrow. There is nothing to be gained by remaining on here, and Cardozo is staying with my father till I relieve him. I am winding up my affairs, and paying off my servants, except Jan Mahomed, and his son, who are coming with me, and to-morrow I turn my back upon Shirani."

"Short—sharp—and decisive is the word," sneered Waring, with bitter emphasis. "Have you got over your good-byes yet?" he added, with pitiless significance.

"No," becoming rather white, "not yet."

"I was told at the club that you were engaged to her. Is *she* to form part of the new scheme? Will marrying her also come under the head of the 'right thing to do?' Eh?"

"You may spare your gibes," said Jervis, sternly. "Miss Gordon is absolutely free. As for myself—I shall never marry."

"Oh, ho!" with a derisive laugh, "never is a long word. Well, to descend to more prosaic matters, what about these Shirani bills and that five hundred?"

"You shall have it, of course."

"Yes, you are a man of your word, even if it is a question of a thrashing. I'll never forget the day that the cad who was ill-using a horse on the towing-path riled you and taunted you; he got hold of the wrong man that time, and no mistake, poor beggar. He never guessed how you could use your fists. You looked so slim and genteel, but you left him with two lovely black eyes."

Mark made a gesture of protest. Time was precious. What was the use of raking up irrelevant old stories?

"Can't you draw upon the uncle for a couple of thousand, at least?" urged Waring, after a considerable silence; "it will be no more to him than a couple of pence—and will save me from—from——"

"What?" asked his companion quietly.

"From," avoiding his penetrating eye, "a lot of bother and worry."

"I cannot draw on him now for a penny, beyond the five hundred; but I am sure he will help you when you see him. How soon are you going home?"

"In a week. Hullo!" starting up, "there is the mess bugle. Are you coming over to dinner?"

"No; tell the mess sergeant to send me something."

"Any champagne? I'd recommend a bottle of the pink wine of France. You are bound to see things more *couleur de rose*."

Jervis shook his head with an air of impatient negation.

"Well, I must go and change; but I'll look you up again, of course, before you turn in."

Clarence proved as good as his word; besides, he had as yet to receive a certain sum of money. He duly appeared about eleven o'clock, unusually flushed, and in a state of boisterous good humour. He found his former comrade still sitting at their joint writing-table, scribbling notes and servants' chits.

"You look as if you were making out your last will and testament. Writing your own obituary notice, eh, old chappie?"—slapping him familiarly on the back. "In one sense you *are* committing suicide, and burying yourself alive. I've sold your chestnut pony, and got the cheque—two fifty rupees—dirt cheap."

"It will go towards paying off some of these," said Mark, nodding at the bills.

"Oh, a mere drop in the ocean," rejoined Clarence, with easy scorn. "However, we can't have our cake and eat it," ignoring the fact that it was he who had devoured not only his own cake, but the other man's as well.

"Here is the cheque for five hundred pounds," said Mark, producing his cheque-book. "I told Uncle Dan I was going to draw it some time ago, so it will be all right"—writing rapidly and handing it over. "It will clear all bills here—mess, rent, and shops; or"—still retaining it— "shall *I* keep it and pay them? I can send the money by post."

Waring glanced at the slip of paper held towards him. His eyes blazed with a curious light; his voice was husky as he eagerly answered, "No, no; you may rely on me. I'll be paymaster to the very end of the chapter," and he seized upon the cheque somewhat precipitately.

"And you will not make any other use of it than paying off our joint debts? You will promise me that, Clarence?" speaking with an air of cool authority. "On your honour, Waring?"

"On my word and honour. What do you take me for, old man? I'll get it cashed at the treasury here, pay all the bills like a gentleman, and send you the receipts. I hope that will please you?"

"Yes, that will do, of course; and mind you settle them at once."

"I hear old Double Gloster and Miss Paske are engaged," said Clarence, hastily changing the subject.

"Are they?" indifferently. What was Shirani news to him now?

"And there is not a road in India wide enough for Aunt Ida. Well, Mark, I am sorry you are so headstrong. You were always a bit hard in the mouth, though you never kicked over the traces. You've been a brick, I must say. What time are you off to-morrow?"

"About seven o'clock."

"Then I think I'll say good night. You look pretty fagged, and you had better turn in. This"—nodding—"is not good-bye; I'll make a point of seeing you in the morning."

Nevertheless Mark stood erect, and held out his hand in silence.

How pale he looked; how worn and haggard he had become! Clarence intuitively felt that this was their last interview; something indefinable assured him that they would never again stand face to face.

He was conscious of an extraordinary mixture of regret and relief. Jervis had represented a sort of conscience. His example, his disagreeably rigorous standard of honour, his steady eyes, had shamed him from doing many things that he ought not to have done. Mark was a young saint, a hero; yes, Miss Valpy was right, he had the face of one. It was the act of a hero to renounce the world, wealth, and love—occasionally synonymous with the flesh and the devil—and devote his life to a crazy old man. He was a cool, reliable comrade, ready with tongue, arm, or rifle. It was true that he had been the means of pulling him out of several nasty scrapes, and this cheque for five hundred pounds, now in his waistcoat pocket, would pull him out of the worst scrape of all!

He waited until he saw Mark go into his room and close the door, and then he slipped back to the club to play "snookers" and black pool. He was not home until three o'clock in the morning; and when he awoke about noon, and shouted for his bearer and his tea, he was informed that the "chotah sahib," as the servants called Jervis, "had been gone many hours."

CHAPTER XXXVI.
"GOOD-BYE FOR EVER! GOOD-BYE, GOOD-BYE!"

It was about eight o'clock in the morning, and Mrs. Brande, as she put the last touches to her toilet, was certain that she heard a man's (a gentleman's) voice in the verandah. Pelham was from home; who could it be at such an hour? Some one come for "Chotah Hazree." Well, Honor would look after him! Ten minutes later she came out, flourishing in her hand a freshly unfolded handkerchief, and gave quite a little gasp of pleasure as she recognized Mark Jervis. He was leaning against the stone pillar of the verandah talking earnestly to her niece, and his pony was waiting at the steps.

"Why, I do declare, this *is* a pleasure," she cried; "a sight for sore eyes! Where have you been hiding yourself this ten days?"

But somehow her exuberant delight was instantly quenched, when she caught sight of the faces of the two young people. Mark looked strangely agitated and as if he had but just recovered from some all but mortal sickness. Honor, her bright, happy Honor, was as smileless and white as death.

"I have come," said Jervis, advancing with an outstretched hand, "to say good-bye."

"Dear, dear, dear!" waving away his salute. "You have not said, 'How do you do?' to me yet!"

"No, I'm afraid I am very stupid to-day. I don't intend to have any secrets from you, Mrs. Brande."

"Oh, I know your secret, so does every one," nodding. "I think you might have given us a *little* hint."

"You mean about the money; and I would have done so only my hands were tied."

"And your cunning cousin never let on!"

"No, but that is not what I have to tell you——"

"Then come into the drawing-room and sit down like a Christian, and send the pony round."

He shook his head emphatically as he said, "I can only wait a short time. I am going off now to a place forty miles away, to live with my father."

"Your father!" she repeated, incredulously.

"Yes, my uncle adopted me when my father married again. My father is Major Jervis, he has lived in these hills for some years. I never knew his whereabouts until recently. The night of the ball he sent for me, he believed that he was dying, and I went off at once—I found him very ill, and quite alone and desolate. I am going to keep him company for the rest of his days. You see, he has no one in the world belonging to him but me."

"Well, I declare!" said Mrs. Brande, after a pause. "It is awfully good of you, that I will say; but if you are your uncle's adopted son, how will *he* take it?"

"Badly, I am afraid, but I cannot be in two places; my uncle has a wife, and heaps of friends, and money, and first rate health."

"Make your father come in to Shirani; we will put him up; and why not get him to go home?"

"It would be of no use to urge him to either step; he is a fixture in his present home for as long as he lives."

"Well, at least you will often come in and see us—*you* are not a fixture!" she urged eagerly.

"Mrs. Brande, you are very good—I shall never forget all your kindness to me—but as far as I can see, I shall never come back to Shirani again. My father could not spare me, for one thing—and for another," and there was a ring of passion in his voice as he added, "I could not endure it. Think of me, as companion to an invalid, with every moment occupied," and here his words sounded a little husky. "Do not tempt me."

"Oh, Mark, my boy, I am so sorry!" she exclaimed; "to think that this is good-bye—that we shall not see you again."

Mark told himself that this so-called underbred, vulgar woman had accepted the news of the shattering of her niece's fortune in a manner that no duchess could have surpassed. Apparently it was not the loss of position, of thousands a year, that had cut her up—she had stood that with marvellous stoicism—it was the loss of Mark himself!

"You know, of course, what my hopes were," he said, glancing towards Honor, who stood at the far end of the verandah, gazing out at what—? "There is an end to them now. Some explanation is due to you and Mr. Brande, and I will write. She need never know *all.* Let people in Shirani suppose what they please, as long as it does not reflect on *her.* Our engagement was never given out—it was a mere matter of hours. My father is peculiar, he wishes to keep his name and existence a secret—you will understand all—later on."

"I remember him well," said Mrs. Brande; "such a handsome fellow, and so fond of society, and so popular. His second wife—I have seen her—a dark person, with——Well, she is dead; let her rest. Oh, Mark, I suppose this must be. But is there not some way out of this trouble, some loophole, some alternative? Surely you would not sacrifice my poor Honor and yourself for nothing?" And her still pretty blue eyes swam in tears.

"No, Mrs. Brande, you may rely on me in that. To hold to Honor—I give up Honor. May she come as far as the gate with me?"

"Yes, she may, to be sure."

"And give me something—you have no photograph, I know—just to show that we part friends?" And he looked at her appealingly.

Mrs. Brande, who had been crying, deliberately wiped her eyes, and threw both her arms round his neck and kissed him. It was no mere playful threat this time! The dirzee, who had just arrived, and was slowly unfolding his mat, could hardly believe his senses. He told the scandal in the bazaar that evening, and was laughed to scorn for his pains!

The young couple, closely followed by syce and pony, walked slowly to the gate; ay, and up the road.

"I little thought how I should next see you, and what I should have to tell you, when we last parted at this very gate," he said at last.

"You are giving up a fortune and great prospects, I know, Mark, because you find your duty lies out here; you are giving up the world and going into banishment. But, Mark, I prepare you, that I am going to say something"—with a catch of her breath—"that may lower me in your eyes; still I will venture. Surely you need not give up *me*. Please"—speaking forcibly—"hear my reasons. I am accustomed to a very quiet life at home. I was brought up in poverty; I shall make a capital poor man's wife. You say your father's affairs are in a fearful muddle, and that he has but an annuity. I can nurse him, read to him, walk out with him, and amuse him; I will be very good to your father. I don't want society, or new dresses, or anything, or any one—but you, Mark. I know that I am shamefully bold and unmaidenly—it would kill Mrs. Grundy to hear me—but I believe you think that I shall mind your dull, lonely jungle life; that I shrink from poverty. You are quite mistaken; I shall enjoy it with you. Do not say 'No,' Mark, even if we must wait. I am ready to wait—ten, twenty years—thirty years," concluded this reckless young woman.

She was waiting now for his answer, white and trembling from the force of her own emotion.

"Honor, I know you will pity me," he began at last, "pity me, when I tell you that I must say 'No.' I must face this life alone. God bless you, and give you a double share of happiness—your own, and what might have been mine. I have lately learnt something"—and his pale face grew ashy grey—"that will prevent my ever calling any woman 'wife.' The sacrifice I am bound to make is bitter; yes, bitter as death. I am not going to sacrifice you; you must forget me, darling. You have all your young life before you; put me out of your mind—gradually, sorrowfully, tenderly—as if I was dead."

"I shall never do that, Mark. Tell me; may I write to you?"

"No!" was the most unexpected and chilling reply.

"But yes, as your sister?" she pleaded, boldly.

He shook his head.

"I could never come to think of you as my sister."

"At least you will give me your address? Once, we were to have spent our lives together; now, I may not even know where I am to think of you as spending yours."

"You had much better not think of me at all," he answered, with a tremor in his voice.

"I must, and I shall. Be quick and tell me."

"My father calls himself Mr. Jones; he lives beyond Hawal Ghât, about forty miles away, and I must be with him before dark. By-the-by, I have kept your fan; it may seem an odd notion, but you will understand. And now I must go."

Hearing the sound of clattering hoofs and gay laughing voices rapidly approaching, he held her hand in his but for one second and dropped it. Then the syce hurrying forward with the pony, he mounted and galloped off. No—he never looked back.

Honor stood for a moment as in a sort of trance; then she turned and leaned against the palings, which bordered a pine-forest sloping to the road. The gay riding party cantering past, rather wondered to see Miss Gordon without her hat, evidently looking for something in the wood. They had no time to stop and ask her what it was that she had lost?

They would have been rather astonished if they could have learnt the truth—that she had just that moment lost her lover,—and for ever. They might have guessed at a tragedy of the kind, had they seen her white set face, and the expression of the clenched hands that grasped the palings. But they did not see, nor did they suspect any connection between Miss Gordon looking into a wood, and a momentary vision of a young fellow on a bay pony, who had flashed up a side path, before they could identify either man or beast.

Honor, with a perfectly colourless face, walked up to her aunt, who was still softly sobbing in the drawing-room, and leaning her hand upon her shoulder, said in a strange emotionless voice—

"It is all over, auntie. We have said good-bye for ever."

She stooped and kissed her, and went and shut herself up in her own room, from which she did not emerge for several hours; and then the girl who did appear was a different Honor Gordon.

CHAPTER XXXVII.
THE SON AND THE HEIR.

"I never expected to see you again," cried Fernandez, as with a napkin over his arm, and a lamp held above his round black head, he surveyed Jervis, who was stiffly dismounting from his pony.

"Why not?" inquired the traveller, as he came up the steps.

"*Every* why not, my dear fellow. If I had been in your shoes, you'd never have seen *me* again. I'd have taken my *jawab.* You are a young man in a thousand." And he patted him affectionately on the shoulder.

"Not at all"—following him into the dining-room, where the remains of an excellent repast was on the table—"I'm simply a young man of my word."

Fernandez may have belied himself, but the chances were that his own estimate of his character was correct. There is much in heredity! He came of an easy-going, voluptuous, volatile stock, as his soft fat face, loose mouth, and merry but unsteady eye indicated. His companion was descended from another and stronger nation; his character was cast in a sterner mould; he was the scion of a race of soldiers, who had fought, suffered, and died for a cause. Jervis's square jaw, resolute glance, and firmly-cut thin lips, told a tale of where the flesh had warred against the spirit, and had *not* prevailed.

"How is my father?" he asked, ere he seated himself.

"Perfectly well—that is, his mind. He has been looking for you all day with the spy-glass. He was tired and went to bed early. He said he knew you would be here by morning. If you *had* deserted him, I don't know how it would have been"—touching his forehead significantly.

Fernandez gesticulated incessantly with a pair of small, plump, delicately shaped hands, on which flashed rings of great value, and of which he was equally proud.

He played the part of host to the son of the house, anxiously pressed him to eat dainties, and drink champagne, and was exceedingly loquacious and confidential. The pale and worn-looking traveller ate but little, and supported his share of conversation by monosyllables, whilst Mr. Cardozo discoursed volubly of his late cousin, and threw a somewhat lurid light upon her married life.

"Oh yes, Mércèdes was very generous and hospitable, and not bad looking—no, when she did not disfigure herself with a mask of pearl powder; but she was frightfully extravagant, as intriguing as her grandmother, and as jealous as"—immediate words failed him for a simile, and after a considerable pause, he added—"the devil. No, the poor major had his own troubles. He might not speak to another woman; he was handsome and popular, and had a taking manner; he could not help that. But she made some awful scenes."

"Did she?" returned Jervis, with the provoking indifference of a young man to whom domestic "scenes" are merely a figure of speech.

"Yes, there is a great deal to be said in favour of the zenana system," continued Fernandez, solemnly. "There are no open scandals, no hysterics at balls, no slapping of other ladies at dinner-parties, no making a man look small before his comrades. Mércèdes took good care never to look small herself. She always rented the biggest bungalow in a station, and had it coloured outside to suit her taste—it was generally pink-and-white, like a Christmas cake! She kept open house and about fifty servants. She liked to sit behind four spanking horses—the major was a capital whip. And as to her diamonds—why, she blazed like a catherine-wheel. She left all the jewels to the major for life, as a mockery, for they are no use to him, he cannot sell a stone; but I can, and will, by-and-by. The native jewels are worth lakhs. Most of them are in the bank at Calcutta; but there are a few here in a safe—jewelled daggers, horse pistols, gold battle-axes, betel-boxes. There is one emerald and ruby necklace, with pearl tassels, that is worth fifty thousand rupees, and a sirpesh or forehead ornament, set with huge rubies, said to have belonged to Ahmed, the last native conqueror of India——"

These descriptions were rolling off Fernandez' fluent tongue, when it occurred to him that he was speaking to deaf ears. What would rouse this odd, abstracted young man—the mention of money?

"The jewels, I see, do not interest you," he exclaimed; "but I must tell you something about your father's income."

The abstracted young man turned a pair of steady eyes on the descendant of a Portuguese free lance and nodded assent.

"Mércèdes made her will in a tantrum; she had made and revoked dozens. However, as she was suddenly cut off, this one had to stand. She left me, her sole heir, a fine present income—*everything* at your father's death. He has a thousand pounds a year as long as he lives, or until he marries, and up till now the money is thrown away and wasted; it goes to blood-suckers and hangers-on in hundreds—to every one but the owner. When he has one of his bad attacks, he will draw a cheque for the asking. Unprincipled tradespeople have sent in accounts for articles that have never come here. There are, however, four hundred military saddles in one of the lumber-rooms, and about nine hundred pairs of long jack-boots. He raises a regiment, you see, when he is not in one of his melancholy fits. A great deal of money sticks to Fuzzil's greasy palms."

"So I should suppose; but that is over."

"There is a leper village chiefly supported by the major in his lucid intervals. The beggars and lepers assemble on Sunday for their alms. It is a great charity."

"Yes; which is more than we can say for Fuzzil"—with a mechanical smile.

"Well, I am off to-morrow; my wife is expecting me," continued Cardozo, briskly.

"Then you are married!" exclaimed the other, with unqualified surprise.

"No, I don't look it, do I? But I married when I was eighteen—the more fool I!—to a pretty little girl you could almost blow away. Yes; and now she weighs sixteen stone. She has very bad health, and seldom goes out, though I keep a fine carriage and horses for her. She does not care for anything much, as long as she has her priest, her doctor, her woman cronies, who tell her all the gossip, and her coffee. Oh, she is very particular about her coffee. She is not fond of clothes, or jewellery, or show; indeed, poor woman, she is too unwieldy to dress and go about. Now, *I* am a society man;" and he threw himself back with a smile of extravagant superiority. "I go round looking after the property, I run up to Mussouri often, I have plenty of friends. I do a little betting, I play billiards, I am passionately fond of dancing. I appreciate a good dinner and a pretty woman—and pretty women appreciate *me*. Oh yes!"

He half closed his eyes, and puffed and blinked alternately, with an air of ineffable content. It was all that his *vis-à-vis* could do to keep his countenance; indeed, he was not entirely successful.

"Oh, you may laugh!" exclaimed Mr. Cardozo, with perfect good humour. "Other men laugh, too; but *I* win—I walk in," he concluded, with an air of superb complacency.

Mark gazed dispassionately at his little stout, sleek companion. He was fat and forty, effeminate and vain; but then he was wealthy and good-natured. Were these the traits that appeal most strongly to women-kind?

"I am a great ladies' man, I do assure you. I could show you letters——"

Jervis made a gesture of frantic dissent.

"Bah, bah, bah! Why, you know very well you've had fifty love affairs *yourself*."

"If I had I should keep them to myself."

"That's a snub"—with a roar of laughter. "And you *would*; you are a close sort of fellow, I should say. Now, I am not; I like talking about my experiences."

"With Mrs. Cardozo, of course."

"Mrs. Cardozo knows there is no harm in *me*; but I must have my own friends, just as she has hers." And he stretched out his arm and amorously contemplated a slender gold bangle. "I suppose"—with a self-conscious smile—"you don't possess one?"

"Great aunt! I should think not. Do you wear a necklace, too?"

Mr. Cardozo, who was certainly the soul of good humour, burst into another roar of laughter; and Fuzzil, who was listening at the door, reported that "the Kala Sahib and the other were talking like brothers."

"Well, well; enjoy life while you may—that's *my* motto." And he drank off a bumper of Madeira and smacked his lips audibly. "You need not be shocked; I shall take the best care of Maria as long as she lives, and when she dies I shall marry again—probably a young girl."

Mark offered no comment, none being required.

"Yes, I enjoy life. And you; what will you do here? Wait"—with a dramatic gesture—"I will answer my own question. Either this"—holding a glass to his lips—"or this"—drawing his hand significantly across his throat.

"Satan finds some mischief still

For idle hands to do."

"My hands will be full," rejoined the other resolutely. "I intend to work great reforms. I shall manage the domestic budget; I shall get rid of Fuzzil and his clan."

"Ho, ho, ho! you will just as easily get rid of the sun, moon, and stars. He is a fixture; he has been here for years. His brother is khitmatgar; his father is cook; his uncle is dhobie. Oh, Fuzzil has struck in his roots; he knows when he is well off."

"And I know when we are *not* well off. He is a gambling, drunken, insolent ruffian. Rooted, you say! I shall turn him out, root *and* branch."

"You will be very strong if you do that," rejoined Fernandez, looking between his eyelashes at the spare, stern-faced young man across the table, who continued—

"I will depend on you to send me up a decent cook. I shall put my bearer at the head of the staff; his son will attend my father."

"They will rob you, of course," remarked Cardozo, with a shrug.

"I doubt it. But if they do, it will be in a quiet and respectable manner—not indecently and extravagantly—and to no great extent. The money will pass through my hands. The mallees must learn that they will no longer receive a garden rent free, and wages for working for themselves. We will have some new furniture, the house cleaned and routed out, a daily dâk, papers, books, a pony for my father."

"You will never do all this—never. I wish you every success, you know"—nodding towards him—"but the labours of Hercules, the cleaning of the Augean stables, were a mere joke to your task. Come, now, I'm a sporting fellow; I bet you fifty rupees to twenty, that when I come back in a couple of months' time, just to see if you are alive, I shall find our friend Fuzzil and the goats, old hags, children, and chickens, *in statu quo*."

Jervis shook his head; he was not in the mood to bet or joke. Life was real, life was earnest—grim earnest, with him now.

"Well, ta-ta! it is nearly twelve o'clock, and I have to make an early start," said Mr. Cardozo, rising, and with a yawn that seemed to divide his head in two parts, he waved a valediction with his pet hand and ring, and swaggered off to bed.

But Mark Jervis was of stronger stuff than flabby, emotional, self-indulgent Fernandez; and after a desperate struggle he carried out his plans. The desperate struggle being on the part of his father's good-for-nothing retinue. When in one brief sentence he informed Fuzzil that he no longer required his services, Fuzzil looked as if he could not credit his ears. He blew out his fat cheeks, and struck an attitude of defiance, as with folded arms and head on one side he said—

"You not my master. I take no orders."

"I am your master now," said Jervis.

"I never going. This Mr. Cardozo's house."

"Indeed! I think he would be surprised to hear that; and you will find that you are mistaken. You have made a very good business out of this situation. Your time is up, and you clear out to-morrow."

Mahomed, the bearer, and his following arrived, and a grand transformation scene ensued. Some old women in the compound and stabling had to be carried out bodily, shrieking vociferously, with their beds and cooking things and other luggage—the collection of years of thieving—like so many magpies' nests. Fuzzil himself had also to be assisted off the premises, being extremely drunk, his turban askew, and uttering wild cries of vengeance, with spluttering, foaming mouth. And then the new *régime* came into working order. The house underwent a consolidated spring cleaning; sun and air were admitted to dusty old locked-up rooms—rooms that offered many surprises in the shape of their contents; a mixture of the properties of East and West—old howdahs and silver horse-trappings, rusty swords and spears, images of saints, holy water stands, crucifixes, pictures, tulwars, bonnets, betel-nut boxes, hookahs, armour. It was, in fact, a combination of a native "tosha-khana," or wardrobe room—an oratory and a pawnbroker's shop.

Dust, and dirt, and cobwebs were swept out, as well as goats, and kids, and poultry. House linen, glass, and crockery, and carpets were replaced—money and the telegraph wires can do great things—walls were white-washed, windows cleaned, jungle cut down. Thus was order and energy infused into every department. The "Pela Kothi," though shabby, was neat and cheerful. The meals were good, and served by snowy-clad servants; flowers and fruit were actually to be seen on the table. There was a daily post, books, magazines, and a steady hill pony to carry Major Jervis. But he preferred to hobble on his son's arm a hundred times up and down the terrace, talking of old times, and noting each turn with a bean. He was a different man already, roused at any rate for the moment from his stupor; he took an interest in the news of the day, in the garden, and, above all, in his pensioners, the lepers.

The young reformer, who had been the means of all these changes, had worked hard, worked ceaselessly from morning till night. He felt that incessant occupation was his only refuge; he dared not give himself time to think. He walked over the hills of an afternoon, when his day's work was done, walked until he was so completely worn out that he was safe to sleep like a log, and, above all, safe from what he most dreaded—dreams.

CHAPTER XXXVIII.
THE VOICE IN THE CONDEMNED CANTONMENT.

The condemned cantonment had an extraordinary fascination for Mark Jervis, and he frequently made a considerable detour, in order to return home by the path that led through this beautiful but melancholy spot. The world had abandoned it for a good reason—he had abandoned the world for a good reason, they had something in common in their isolation. He was familiar with the barracks, the mess-house, the ruinous bungalows, their wild tangled gardens, where flower and tree fought desperately against extinction by savage cousins and distant wild relations. Apple and rose trees still managed to hold their own, but heliotrope and geraniums had long succumbed. The churchyard was his constant haunt, he knew the names and short histories on the grave-stones, head-stones, crosses, and not a few immense square tombs, such as appear to be peculiar to old Indian cemeteries. It was as if a small house, or mortuary chapel, had been reared over the departed, and the more sincerely mourned, the larger loomed these great dark weather-stained erections! There was a big and stately edifice dedicated to the memory of Constance Herbert, aged nineteen. What had poor Constance done to deserve to be weighted down with so many tons of masonry? The inscription was effaced. There was another sarcophagus, erected over the remains of a man who was killed by a fall from a precipice; and a tomb, the size of an ordinary gate lodge, was raised to the memory of an infant aged eighteen months.

One evening Mark descended the hill after a long and very erratic tramp; it was the hour of sunset; he stood for a few moments a captive to the influence of his surroundings—the bluish hills, the amethyst-tinted distance, the quiet smokeless bungalows, nestling among their flower-choked verandahs, the soft yellow light flooding the entire valley, the uncanny silence, a silence befitting this forsaken spot.

He sat down on the grass-grown chabootra (or band-stand), drew out and lit a cheroot. It was Sunday, and he instinctively glanced over at the roofless church. What had been the last service held between its walls? A service for the burial of the dead, no doubt—the long-forgotten dead, who were buried in its precincts. As he sat there alone in the midst of dumb witnesses of the past, his mind travelled back over his whole life, and he steadily reviewed its most memorable incidents one by one; the most noteworthy of all had befallen him in these very mountains. His thoughts dwelt on his uncle, then on Honor Gordon. What was she doing just now? Perhaps she was sitting in church, listening attentively to one of Mr. Paul's brief and excellent sermons. Had her thoughts, or prayers, ever strayed to him? Was it true what Miss Paske had said about woman's thoughts? Could he honestly tell his own heart that he hoped Honor Gordon had forgotten him? Would he prefer to be what the Bible terms "a dead man, out of mind?"

The sun had drawn away his bright warm cloak foot by foot, the grey pall of a short Indian twilight was rapidly spreading over the valley. Shadows advanced stealthily and momentarily, the woods were inscrutable, and the first cry of the jackal rose through the sharp hill air.

Jervis had risen already to depart, when his attention was arrested by an unexpected sound—no jackal this, it was a voice, a human voice—coming from the direction of the church or churchyard. He almost held his breath to listen, and this is what he heard, in what had been once a full rich contralto. Every syllable was distinctly audible, and there was a slight almost imperceptible pause between each word—

"Oh, where shall rest be found—

Rest for the weary soul?

'Twere vain the ocean's depths to sound,

Or pierce to either pole."

There was a silence of a full minute, during which the young man's heart thumped loudly against his ribs. Was he listening to the voice of one risen from the grave?

Then the weird singing recommenced, with a wail of passionate despair in the notes—

"The world can never give

The bliss for which we sigh;

'Tis not the whole of life to live,

Nor all of death to die."

He waited for a considerable time in a fever of thrilling expectancy—but there was no more. Having made certain of this, his next move was to acquaint himself with the personality of the performer. He ran over to the ruins of the church, climbed in across a pile of broken masonry—the small square enclosure was easily measured at one glance—it was empty.

Then he walked slowly round, and examined the walls by the dying light. No, his quest was vain, there was not a soul—undoubtedly it had been a soul—

to be seen. In the gathering darkness, the now silent valley had grown very sombre, the trees made awful shadows, and the forest seemed to stretch away up the mountains, until it was lost in the dusky sky.

"In what direction did you ride to-day, Mark?" inquired his father as they sat over their dessert.

"I cannot tell you precisely, sir; but I came home by the cantonment."

"A lovely spot; the authorities could not have chosen better, if they had searched five hundred miles—good air, good water, good aspect; and yet the last regiment died there like flies. The natives say it is an accursed place, and not a man of them will go near it after sundown."

"I suppose you don't believe in that sort of thing, sir; you are not superstitious?"

"Not I," indignantly. "Mércèdes was superstitious enough for fifty; she had all the native superstitions at her finger-ends, and the European ones to boot! There was very little scope left between the two! Almost everything you said, or did, or saw, or wore, was bound to have a meaning, or to be an omen, or to bring bad luck. I remember she was reluctant to start from Mussouri the day she met her death, simply because she found a porcupine's quill upon the doorstep! I have seen some queer things in my day," continued Major Jervis. "When we were quartered at Ameroo I got a fright that I did not recover from for months. I had lost my way out pig-sticking, and was coming back alone, pretty late. At one part of the road I had to pass a large irregular strip of water, and there standing upright in the middle of it was actually a *skeleton*, swaying slowly to and fro; I shall never forget that blood-curdling sight—and I don't know how I got home, to this very day."

"And how was it accounted for?"

"By perfectly natural causes, of course! Cholera had broken out at a village close to where I saw the spectre, and the people had died in such numbers that there was no time for the usual funeral pyre. It was as much as those spared could do to bring the corpse to the spot, tie a gurrah (those large water vessels) to head and feet, fill them with water, push the body out, and then turn and fly almost before it could sink out of sight! My ghost was one of these bodies. The gurrah from the head had broken away, and that at the feet had pulled the corpse into an upright position, and there it was, a spectacle to turn a man's brain! We were quartered at Ameroo for four years, and I never passed that miserable spot without a shudder. When I last saw it the water lay low, covered with the usual reddish-looking Indian water-weed;

down by the edge was a skull blackening in the sun. That hideous pool was the grave of two hundred people."

"And so your ghost was accounted for and explained away," said Mark. "Did you ever come across anything, in all your years out here, that could *not* be accounted for or explained away?"

"Yes, I did; a queer, senseless, insignificant little fact, as stubborn as the rest of its tribe. One morning many years ago I was out pigeon-shooting with some fellows, and we came upon a large peepul tree, among the branches of which waved sundry dirty little red-and-white flags, and under its shade was a chabootra, about fifteen feet square, and raised three feet off the ground. Mounting this, in spite of the protest of a fakir, we discovered a round hole in the centre, and looking down, we perceived filthy water, covered with most unwholesome-looking scum. The sides of the well were hollow and uneven and had a sort of petrified appearance. We asked the reason of the signs of "poojah" we beheld, and heard the simple story of the water in the well. It never increased or decreased, no matter if the weather were hot and dry, or cold and wet; no matter whether rain fell in torrents, or the land was parched with drought, whether sugar-cane juice or the blood of the sacrificial goat was poured in by buckets full, or not at all. It might be closely watched, to show that it was not regulated by human hands, and it would be seen that it never changed. Therefore it was holy. The god "Devi" was supposed to be responsible for the curious phenomenon of the water always standing at the same level—about four feet from the mouth of the well, and never increasing its depth—said to be thirty feet. Over and over again I revisited the spot, so did others—and we never discovered any change. That was a fact we could not explain. All the same, I do not believe in the supernatural!"

As his father did not believe in the supernatural and was likely to be a sceptical listener, Mark resolved to keep his experience to himself; perhaps there might be a natural cause for *it* too.

The arrival of a visitor to the Yellow House was not lost upon the neighbourhood; several young planters flocked down to look him up, and discussed fruit crops, tea crops, and the best beats for gurool, the best rivers and lakes for mahseer, and gave him hearty invitations to their respective bungalows. The German missionary sought him out, also Mr. Burgess the American doctor and padré, who worked among the lepers. He, like his predecessors, had been struck with the remarkable and almost magical change that had been wrought in and around the Pela Kothi. He beheld his patient, Major Jervis, in a comfortable airy room, dressed in a neat new suit, reading a recent *Pioneer* like a sane man. Like a sane man, he discussed politics, local topics, and with greater enthusiasm his son, who unfortunately was not at home. Presently an excellent tiffin was served to the visitor, he was conducted round the garden, and as he noted the improvements in every department, he came to the conclusion that Jervis, junior, must be a remarkable individual. He had an opportunity of judging of him personally before he left, for he rode up just as Mr. Burgess was taking his departure, regretted that he had not arrived sooner, and calling for another pony, volunteered to accompany the reverend guest part of the way home.

A spare resolute-looking young fellow and a capital rider, noted Mr. Burgess, as Mark's young pony performed a series of antics all the way down the path in front of his own sober and elderly animal.

"Your father is wonderfully better. I am his medical adviser, you know," said the missionary.

"Yes, and I wish you lived nearer than twelve miles."

"He has a wonderful constitution. He has had one stroke of paralysis, he may be taken suddenly, and he may live for the next thirty years. Is it long since you met?"

"I have not seen him till lately—since I was a child."

"That is strange, though of course India does break up families."

"I was adopted by an uncle, and lived in London most of my time."

"Ah, I understand; and came out to visit your father."

"Yes, partly; indeed, I may say chiefly."

"And have thrown in your lot with him. Mr. Jervis, I honour you for it." Mark looked uncomfortable, and his companion added, "This life must be a great change, indeed, as it were another form of existence, to you; you must not let yourself stagnate now you have set your house in order, but come among us when you can. There are Bray and Van Zee, the two nearest planters to you, both good fellows. You have a much nearer neighbour, that you will never see."

"Indeed, I am sorry to hear that. May I ask why?"

"It is one who shrinks from encountering Europeans, even holds aloof from me. Though we work in the same field, we have rarely met."

Mark would have liked to have gleaned more particulars, but the burly American missionary was not disposed to be communicative, and all he could gather about his mysterious neighbour was, that the individual was not a European, not a heathen, and not young.

CHAPTER XXXIX.
A FRIENDLY VISIT.

Captain Waring had departed for England without ceremony or beat of drum (leaving his debts behind him), also presumably his cousin, who had not had the common decency to leave P. P. C. cards—no, not even on the mess or the club—and who had treated poor Honor Gordon shamefully; indeed, several matrons agreed that in the good old days such a man would certainly have been shot or horsewhipped!

How Colonel Sladen had chuckled, surmised, and slandered, had bemoaned the girl's lost good looks, and her aunt's idiotcy to all comers, as he waited impatiently for his afternoon rubber! Next to his whist, the relaxation he most thoroughly enjoyed was a *bonâ fide* ill-natured gossip, with a sauce in the form of sharp and well-spiced details.

No reliable information respecting Mr. Jervis had as yet been circulated—for Clarence, on second thoughts, had kept his late comrade's plans and whereabouts entirely to himself.

Mrs. Brande knew, and held her tongue. What was the good of talking? She was much subdued in these days, even in the colour of her raiment. She rarely went to the club; she dared not face certain questioning pitiless eyes in the awful verandah; indeed she kept in the background to an unparalleled degree. Nevertheless she had her plans, and was prepared to rise phoenix-like from the ashes of her former hopes. She was actually contemplating a second venture, in the shape of a niece. She thought Honor wanted cheering up, and a face from home—especially such a lovely face—would surely have a happy result. But Honor's thoughts were secretly fixed upon another countenance, a certain colourless, handsome face—a face she never expected to see again. Her mind dwelt with poignant memories on a pair of eyes, dim with wordless misery, that had looked into her own that hateful June morning.

"We can well afford it, P.," urged his wife, apropos of her scheme. "One girl is the same as two—one ayah between them." She little knew Fairy.

"Please yourself," cried Mr. Brande, at last; "but Honor shall always be my niece, my chief niece, and nothing shall ever put her nose out of joint with her uncle Pelham."

"No one wants to! I should like to see any one try that, or with me either. But what a nose Fairy has! Just modelled to her face like a wax-work."

Mrs. Brande talked long and enthusiastically to Honor about her sister. But Honor was not responsive; her eyes were averted, her answers unsatisfactory; indeed, she said but little, and looked positively uncomfortable and distressed. And no doubt she felt a wee bit guilty because she had prevented the child from coming out before. But that was very unlike Honor; Mrs. Brande could not understand it.

How she would exult in a niece who was a miracle of loveliness, instead of being merely a pretty, bright, and popular girl. Not that Honor was very bright now; she was losing her looks, and Honor's love affair had come to such a woeful end. Honor was not the sort of girl to take up with any one else; and, indeed, she could not wonder. Poor Mark! of all her boys, he was the one nearest to her heart.

Still she considered that he had carried filial love a great deal too far, when she had thought over his sacrifice in moments of cool reflection. It was a shame that Mark, and Honor, and a magnificent fortune should all be sacrificed to an eccentric old hermit.

Mrs. Brande said little; she was not receiving the support and encouragement she expected. She placed Fairy's photograph in poor Ben's silver frame in a conspicuous place in the drawing-room, and she mentally sketched out the rough draft of another letter to Hoyle.

Before this letter took definite shape, Mrs. Langrishe came to call—a dinner "call"—in full state and her best afternoon toilet. Seating herself on the sofa, she began to tell Mrs. Brande all about her dear invalid, exactly as if she were talking to a most sympathetic listener—instead of to a deadly rival.

"He is such a nice man, and so quiet in a house."

"For that matter," retorted Mrs. Brande, "he is quiet enough out of the house, and everywhere else."

"And he is so contented and easily amused," continued Mrs. Langrishe. "I left him with Lalla reading aloud to him."

"Do you think that is *quite* the thing?" inquired Mrs. Brande, with a dubious sniff.

"Why should she not do it as well as hospital nurses?" demanded her visitor.

Mrs. Brande reflected on the result of her own nursing. Would this nursing have the same effect?

"Hospital nurses are generally young, single, and very frequently pretty," resumed Mrs. Langrishe. "They read to their patients, and take tea with them, and no one says a word. All the difference between them and these girls is, their uniform and their experience; and surely *no* one ever dreams of making a remark about those excellent, devoted young women!"

Lalla was not excellent, but she had certainly been most devoted—as her aunt thankfully acknowledged.

"Well, I don't know that I should allow Honor to do it," said Mrs. Brande, with a meditative air.

"Possibly not. It would, of course, depend upon circumstances. Now"—laying two fingers playfully on Mrs. Brande's round arm—"I am going to be a little bird, and whisper a little secret in your ear."

Mrs. Brande drew back, as if she thought Mrs. Langrishe was going to be a little rattlesnake.

"It is not to be given out for a few days, but Lalla and Sir Gloster are engaged. It is quite settled."

Sir Gloster had only proposed the previous evening, and had begged that the fact of the engagement might be kept quiet for a week, until he had wired home to his all-important mother. She must be told before any one. Yes, he had succumbed to Lalla's bright blandishments. He was a dull, heavy man; he liked to be amused. He would have amusement all day long when Lalla was his wife. She had a charming voice, and read aloud well. She brought him all the scraps of news, she was an admirable mimic, an adroit flatterer, and altogether a charming girl; and her daily *tête-à-têtes* were of a most stimulating character, and he looked forward to them with keen anticipation. She gave him a capital description of the unmasking of Captain Waring, the sensation created by the *soi-disant* poor relation; how every one was certain that it was going to be a match between him and Miss Gordon; how he had absconded, and Miss Gordon was left. He had evidently joined his friend in Bombay—*wise* young man!

Sir Gloster, who was naturally of a huffy and implacable disposition, had never recovered the shock to his affections and self-esteem. He was by no means sorry to hear that in her turn Miss Gordon had been spurned, and he was resolved to show her how speedily *he* had been consoled.

Mrs. Langrishe, when she entered Mrs. Brande's house, had not intended to divulge her great news—merely to throw out hints, draw comparisons, and trample more or less on the fallen and forsaken.

But for once human nature was too strong for her: she would have had a serious illness if she had not then and there relieved her mind of her overwhelming achievement.

Mrs. Brande opened her blue eyes to their widest extent; her worst fears were confirmed.

She however mustered up an artificial smile, and said—

"I am sure you are very pleased," which was true—"and I am glad indeed to hear it," which was not true.

"It is to be kept quiet for a week," murmured Mrs. Langrishe; "but I am telling you as an old friend, who I feel *sure* will be pleased with the news. Of course, we are all delighted; it is everything we could wish," and she drew herself up.

"I should rather think it was!" rejoined Mrs. Brande, tartly; she was but human after all.

"My brother and all my people will be much gratified—Sir Gloster is such a dear good fellow, and so well off, and *so* steady."

"I hope he won't be a little *too* steady for Lalla!"

"Not he; and he delights in all her fun, and singing——"

"And dancing?" suggested Mrs. Brande, significantly.

"It will not be a long engagement," ignoring this little thrust. "This is the second week of September; we shall all be going down in another six weeks. We will have the wedding in about a month."

It was on the tip of Mrs. Brande's tongue to say, "Delays are dangerous," but she closed her lips.

"Where is Honor?" inquired Mrs. Langrishe, with rare effusion.

"She has gone off down the khud to get ivy for the table. I have a small dinner this evening."

"You are always having dinners, you wonderful woman."

"Well, you see, in Pelham's *position*, we must entertain, and I make it a rule to have a dinner once a week."

"You are quite a providence to the station!" cried her visitor affectedly. "How pretty those grasses are. I suppose Honor arranged them? What a useful girl she is!"

"Yes, she takes all trouble off my hands. I don't know how I shall ever get on without her."

"How lucky for you, that there is no chance of her *leaving* you! My dear, that was a most unfortunate affair about Mr. Jervis."

"What do you mean?" inquired Mrs. Brande, whose crest began to rise.

"Oh," with a disagreeable laugh, "it is what did *he mean*! He paid Honor the most devoted attention, and the moment he was revealed in his true colours—he fled. No one knows what has become of him."

"Pardon me—*we* do!" returned his champion, with a quiver of her double chin.

"And—where is he, dear? what is he doing?"

"He is doing a good—a noble action. Putting himself and his wishes aside for the sake of others," returned Mrs. Brande in a white heat of emotion.

"Oh well," rather disconcerted, "if you and Honor, and above all *Mr. Brande*, are satisfied, of course there is no more to be said——"

"No," pointedly. "I hope no more will *be* said. Have you seen the photograph of my other niece, Honor's sister?" making a desperate effort to rally and change the conversation, and reaching for the frame, which she solemnly placed in Mrs. Langrishe's hand.

"What do you think of her?" Here at least she was certain of scoring a small triumph.

"Think, my dear woman! Why, that she is perfectly lovely." (It was safe to praise a girl who was in England.)

"At first she was coming out to me," her aunt pursued, "but she changed her mind. Now we are thinking of having her out in November with the Hadfield's girl."

"Indeed," said Mrs. Langrishe, reflectively, and still nursing the picture, as it were, on her knee.

She had a wonderful knack of picking up odd bits of news, and her brain contained useful little scraps of the most promiscuous description. Her mind was a sort of ragbag, and these scraps often came in appropriately. She rummaged out a scrap now.

She had recently heard, from a cousin of hers (an artist), of a Mrs. Gordon, a widow with two daughters, one of them lovely, who was sitting to him as Rowena—an ideal Rowena—but who was also a dwarf—a sort of little creature that you might exhibit.

"Does your niece live at Hoyle, and is her name Fairy?"

"Yes. Why do you ask?" rather eagerly.

"I have heard of her, recently, from my cousin, Oscar Crabbe. And why did she not come out?" looking at her with a queer smile.

"Her health was not very good—and there was some other reason—which I have not been told."

"I know the reason, and can tell you, if you like," said Mrs. Langrishe, with an air of affectionate confidence.

Here was an unexpected opportunity of planting a dart in her adversary's side.

"There is no object in keeping the matter secret, it is just as foolish as that scheme of young Jervis's, who was like an ostrich sticking his head in the sand. By the way, it appears that *that* is quite an exploded idea! Every one in Hoyle knows Miss Fairy Gordon's appearance—she is extraordinary lovely—but——"

"But not mad? Don't say she is mad!" protested Mrs. Brande, excitedly.

"No, no; not so bad as that. But," looking steadily into her listener's eyes, she added, "poor little creature, she is a *dwarf*! She never grew after she was ten, I am told. Yes, it is a dreadful pity," gazing into her hostess's horrified countenance. "Sitting down, she is just like other people—but when she stands up, she seems to have no legs."

"A dwarf! No legs! And she thought of coming to me! And I was just going to write and ask her to start in November," repeated Mrs. Brande in gasps.

"Well, my dear, it is a most fortunate circumstance that your letter has not gone. What could you have done with her? You could never have taken her out except *after dark*."

This was a terribly effective thrust. Mrs. Brande was wholly unable to retaliate, and made no reply.

"A dwarf!" Her mind conjured up a little fat sallow woman, such as she had once seen outside a show at a fair, and that miserable stunted native who was carried about Shirani, begging, on the shoulders of a boy.

And her niece, of whose picture she was so proud, that she had placed it in a solid silver frame—her lovely niece was like that!

"I wonder Honor never told me," murmured Mrs. Brande at last.

"And I do not," was the emphatic rejoinder. "From all accounts, the mother and sisters have always spoiled the little one, who believes that she is in no way different to other people, and is too ridiculously vain. Even if she had been five foot six, I am sure that you are far happier without her," concluded

Mrs. Langrishe, rising and squeezing her hostess's hand as she spoke. And having offered this small fragment of consolation, she rustled away.

Mrs. Brande, poor woman, had been indeed trampled upon, and crushed to the very earth. She had been asked to join in her rival's song of triumph over Miss Paske's superb success; she had been condoled with on her own dear girl's misfortunes; and she had been informed that she was aunt to a dwarf!

She sat for some time in a shattered, stupefied condition; then she got up, and hastily carried off Fairy's photograph and locked it away in a box, secure from all eyes, and from even the ayah's inquisitive brown fingers.

Honor noticed the absence of her sister's picture from its usual post of honour—it was nowhere to be seen—the absence of Fairy's name in conversation, the sudden cessation of all interest in Gerty Hadfield's movements, and guessed rightly that some one had kindly enlightened her aunt, and that she was in possession of the *other* reason now.

CHAPTER XL.
THE NEW WEARER OF THE CORNELIAN RING.

Six weeks had crawled by. With all his occupation Mark found time desperately hard to kill; he felt as if he had lived his present life for at least six years. The monsoon had broken, and on some days the torrents compelled him to remain indoors; and whilst sheets of rain and hurricanes of wind swept the valley, an appalling loneliness settled down upon the miserable young man. His father passed many hours in sleep, and he had not a soul with whom to exchange a word. One evening, during a welcome break, he was riding homewards down a steep and slippery path that wound through wet dark pine-woods, when his pony suddenly shied so violently as almost to lose its footing; he had taken fright at an undefined object beside the road, something which at first his rider mistook for a bear, until it emitted a groan of unmistakable human anguish.

"What is the matter?" asked Jervis, as he quickly dismounted.

"Alas, I have hurt my foot!" replied a female voice in Hindostani. "I fell down—I cannot walk."

Jervis threw the bridle over his arm, lit a match, and, shading it with his hand, saw, huddled up, what appeared to be an old native woman. She explained to him, between groans and gasps, that she had twisted her ankle over a root on the path, and could not move.

"Are you far from home?" he inquired.

"Three miles."

"In which direction?"

"The hill above the old cantonment."

"I know. If you think you can sit on my pony, I will lead him and take you home safely."

"Oh, I am such a coward," she cried. "Is the pony gentle?"

"Yes, he is all right; I will answer for the pony."

"I—and I cannot bear pain. Oh—oh! but I must"—vainly struggling to rise, and sinking down again.

She proved a light weight, as Jervis raised her bodily in his arms, and placed her in the saddle. Fortunately the pony, who bore the suggestive name of "Shaitan," was too much sobered by a long journey to offer any active opposition to carrying a lady. The homeward progress proved exceedingly tedious; the road was bad and nearly pitch dark. The native woman, who appeared to know every yard of the way, directed her companion by a path almost swallowed up in jungle, to a hill behind the old mess-house. Up and up they climbed, till they came to a tiny stone bungalow, with a light in the window. The door was thrown open by another native woman and an old man, whose shrill voluble lamentations were almost deafening.

"You had better let me carry you in?" suggested Jervis.

"No, no." Then imperiously to the other woman, "Anima, bring hither a chair and help me down."

But Anima, of the lean and shrivelled frame, had been set a task far beyond her strength, and in the end it was the muscular arms of the young Englishman that lifted the other from the saddle. As he placed her carefully on the ground, her shawl, or saree, fell back, and the lamplight revealed a fair-skinned woman with snow-white hair, and a pair of magnificent black eyes. She was possibly fifty years of age—or more—and though her lips were drawn with pain, she was remarkably handsome, with a high-bred cast of countenance. No native this; at any rate, she resembled no native that Jervis had ever seen. Who was she?

A glance into the interior surprised him still further; instead of the usual jumble of cooking-pots, mats, and hookahs, he caught a glimpse of a round table, with a crimson cover. A newspaper, or what looked like one, lay upon it; there was an armchair, a fire blazing in a fireplace, with a cat sedately blinking before it.

Who was this woman? He was not likely to learn any further particulars—at present, for she was helped in by her two servants; and as he waited, the door was abruptly closed and barred, and he was left outside, alone in the cold and darkness. Here was gratitude!

He rode slowly home, the pony figuratively groping his way, whilst his master was lost in speculation. This was the mysterious neighbour, he felt certain; this was the tender of the graves—the owner of the voice.

He related his adventure to his father whilst they played picquet.

Major Jervis was not half as much surprised as the young man had anticipated—he simply stroked his forehead, a favourite trick of his, and said, with his eyes still fastened on his cards—

"Oh, so you have come across the Persian woman! I so seldom hear of her, I had forgotten her."

"Persian?"

"Yes. She has been in these hills for years, working among the lepers. A fair-skinned woman, with great haunting dark eyes."

"But who is she?" throwing down his cards and looking eagerly at his father.

"She is what I tell you," impatiently—"a Persian; they are generally fair, and I dare say she has been handsome in her day, about thirty years ago. Why are you so interested?"

"Because I have another idea in my head; I believe she is an Englishwoman."

The major's laugh was loud, and sound, and not at all mad.

"She is a Persian—only, of course, you are no judge—and to the very tips of her fingers."

"But what is she doing up here?"

"I would rather you asked her that than I did," was the extremely sane reply. "She is a Christian, I believe, and is working out her sins. I have no doubt she is a woman with a past. You can read it in her eyes. Come, my boy, take up your hand; it's your turn to play."

Mark Jervis, as we know, had not been permitted time or opportunity to read anything, whether referring to past or present, in the Persian's eyes; but this omission was corrected ere long.

One afternoon he noticed a figure, stick in hand, resting on the mess-house steps, as he rode by—a figure which raised the stick, and imperatively summoned him to approach.

It was undoubtedly his recent acquaintance, who pulled the veil further over her head, as she said—

"Sahib, I wish to thank you for your charitable benevolence. Truly, but for you, I should have lain all night in the forest, in the rain, and among the beasts."

"I hope you are better?" he asked, doffing his cap.

"Yea, nearly well. Though I am a stranger to you, I know that you are Jones Sahib's son."

"Major 'Jervis' is his real name. Yes—I am his son."

"I have heard of you," she continued, rather loftily.

"Indeed!"

"From the leper-folk," she added, significantly.

"It is you who keep the graves yonder in order?"

"May be!" was her cautious reply.

"And who sing English hymns in the old church?"

A slight contraction passed over her face as she replied—

"Nay—I am a Persian woman from Bushire. What should I know of thy songs or thy tongue?"

"Then who—can it be?" inquired Jervis, looking at her steadfastly.

"Noble youth—why ask me? A woman from the dead, perchance," she retorted mockingly.

"At least, it is you who do so much good among the sick Pahari-folk and lepers?" he persisted.

"Yea, I am but one—the field is great. Who can fill jars with dew? I would I could do more."

"I believe that were hardly possible."

"As far as these hands go," extending a pair of delicately-shaped members, "I do what I can; but what is one lemon for a whole village to squeeze! If I had a big house that would serve as a hospital, I should have my heart's desire. I am skilled in medicine, so also is my servant; we would have our sick beside us, and could do much—that is my dream. It will never come to pass till the sun shall be folded up and the stars shall fall."

"Surely one of these bungalows would answer. Why not this mess-house?" suggested Jervis generously.

"True; but the sircar would not yield it to me. Already the sircar has given me my abode; and, doubtless, were I to ask for the Mess Khana, they would aver that I was like to the man who, on receiving a cucumber, demanded a tope of mango trees! Moreover this dead station may reawaken once more. Even in *my* memory the merry sahibs and mem sahibs have sojourned here, and held great tamashas; but it is years since they came, and the place, perchance, is forgotten."

"And so you have lived here alone—for years?" said the young man. His remarkably expressive eyes distinctly added the "*Why?*" his tongue refrained from uttering.

"Yea, I have been dead to the world and the roar of strife and life for many moons! If all tales be true—tales whispered even in this empty land—you have forsaken many delights to give your days to the old man, your father? Is it not so?" She looked up with a quick gesture, and her saree fell back.

As Jervis gazed down into the dark eyes turned towards him, he agreed with his father; here was undoubtedly a woman with a past—and a tragic past!

"It is a noble sacrifice," she continued; "but what saith the Koran? 'Whatever good works ye send on for your behoof, ye shall find them with God.' I am old enough to be your mother. I marvel if I had had a son, would he sacrifice himself thus for me—were I of your people, a Feringhee woman, I marvel?" she repeated meditatively, as she put up her hand to draw her veil further over her head.

As she did so, the young man started as he recognized her ring—Honor's cornelian ring. Many a time he had noticed it on her finger, and her peculiar trick of turning it round and round, when in any mental quandary, had been the subject of more than one family jest. How came it to be on the hand of this Mahommedan woman?

She instantly interpreted his glance, and exclaimed—

"You observe my ring. Truly it is of little value—in money—but to me it is beyond price. It was given to me by a maiden I saw but once. Her words were pearls, her lips were rubies, but her music, and her eyes, drew the story of my life from my inmost soul."

"I am sure I know the lady!" cried her listener impetuously, "young—and tall—and beautiful. She plays what you call the sitar. Where did you meet her?"

"Ah, sahib, that is *my* secret," she answered after an expressive pause; "but, lo! I can reveal yours," and she looked at him steadily as she added, "*you love her.*"

"What do you mean?" he stammered. "Why do you say so?" and he coloured up to the roots of his crisp brown hair.

"Of a truth, I read it in your face. It is not for naught that folk call me a magic wallah." And she rose stiffly to depart. "You have abandoned her, I see," she continued, with a flash of her wonderful eyes, "and lo, the fat old mem sahib, her mother, will marry her to some one else! Behold your reward, for doing your duty!" And entirely forgetting her previous quotation from the Koran, with this unpleasant and cynical remark, the Persian made him a profound salaam, and hobbled away.

CHAPTER XLI.
"IT WAS A HYENA."

The rains were over by the middle of August, and Shirani cast off mackintoshes, discarded umbrellas, and society—restless and fluctuating—looked about for some fresh and novel form of out-door amusement.

Among the second-leave arrivals, the most active and enterprising of the new-comers, was a Captain Bevis, the moving power in whatever station he was quartered; the very man for getting up dances, races, and picnics. He was resolved to strike out an entirely original line on the present occasion, and inaugurated a grand joint expedition into the interior—none of your exclusive "family parties," or a petty little "set" of half a dozen couples. No, this sanguine individual actually proposed to move Shirani *en masse*. He had heard of the abandoned cantonment, of Hawal Bagh, galloped over to inspect it with his customary promptitude, and came flying back to the station on the wings of enthusiasm. "It was a perfect spot," this was his verdict; scenery exquisite, good road, good water, lots of bungalows, a mess-house to dance in, a parade ground for gymkanas. Every one must see the place, every one must enjoy a short informal outing, the entertainment to be called the "Hawal Bagh week." Captain Bevis threw himself into the project heart and soul; he invited another hill station to join; he sent out circulars, he collected entries for gymkanas and polo matches, and the names of patronesses for the grand ball at Hawal Bagh. Dead and long-forgotten Hawal Bagh, that was to awake and live once more!

Subscriptions poured in, parties went over to explore, empty houses were allotted, a vast army of coolies was enlisted, the jungle was cut down, the bungalows cleaned up, the very gardens were put in order. A quantity of supplies and cart loads of furniture were soon *en route*, and the servants of Shirani entered into the project with the zeal of the true Indian-born domestic, who hails a change, a "tamasha," anything in the shape of a "feast," with a joy and energy totally unknown to the retainers of the folk in these colder latitudes.

Hospitable Mrs. Brande was to have a house and a house-party. "P." was absent on official business; but, under any circumstances, he would not have been a likely recruit for what he called a "new outbreak of jungle fever." The Dashwoods, the Booles, the Daubenys, the Clovers, were to have a married people's mess. There were also one or two chummeries, which made people look at one another and smile! The bachelors, of course, had their own mess; moreover, there were tents.

Mrs. Langrishe joined neither mess nor chummery, this clever woman was merely coming as the Clovers' guest for two days, and Lalla was Mrs.

Dashwood's sole charge. Mrs. Sladen, of course, stayed with Mrs. Brande, who had been relegated to the old commandant's house, an important-looking roomy bungalow, standing in a great wilderness of a garden and peach orchard. Once or twice during the last twenty years it, and one or two other bungalows, had been let (to the Persian's great annoyance) for a few months in the season to needy families from the plains, who only wanted air, good hill air, and could afford but little else!

Mrs. Brande and her party arrived a whole day before the general public, travelling comfortably by easy stages through great forests of pine, oak, or rhododendron, along the face of bold, bare cliffs, across shallow river-beds, and through more than one exquisite park-like glade, dotted with trees and cattle—naturally, Mrs. Brande kept a suspicious eye on these latter. When the travellers reached their destination, they found that roads had been repaired, lamp-posts and oil lamps erected, the old band-stand was renovated—servants were hurrying to and fro, carrying furniture, shaking carpets, airing bedding and picketing ponies. There were coolies, syces, soldiers, and active sahibs galloping about giving directions. In fact, Hawal Bagh had put back the clock of time, and to a cursory eye was once more the bustling, populous cantonment of forty years ago!

And how did the scanty society who dwelt in those parts relish the resurrection of Hawal Bagh? To the neighbouring poor hill villagers this event was truly a god-send; they reaped a splendid and totally unexpected harvest, and were delighted to welcome the invaders, who purchased their fowl, eggs, grain, milk, and honey.

Mark Jervis beheld the transformation with mingled feelings. He had broken with his old life; most people, if they thought of him at all, believed him to be in England—two months is a long time to live in the memory of a hill station. Honor—she would be at Hawal Bagh—she had not forgotten him yet. He would hang about the hills, that he might catch a distant glimpse of her, or even of her dress. Surely he might afford himself that small consolation.

As for the Persian, she surveyed the troops of gay strangers from her eerie with a mixture of transports and anguish.

It was a fine moonlight night early in September, the hills loomed dark, and cast deep shadows into the bright white valley. The air was languorously soft, the milky way shone conspicuous, and fully justified its Eastern name, "The Gate of Heaven."

There was to be a ball in the old mess-house, and Mark took his stand on the hill and watched the big cooking fires, the lit-up bungalows, the hurrying figures; listened to the hum of voices, the neighing of ponies, the tuning of musical instruments. Could this be really the condemned, deserted cantonment of Hawal Bagh, that many a night he had seen wrapped in deathlike silence? The dance commenced briskly, open doorways showed gay decorations, the band played a lively set of lancers, and a hundred merry figures seemed to flit round and pass and repass; whilst the jackals and hyenas, who had been wont to hold their assemblies in the same quarter, slunk away up the hills in horrified disgust. Presently people came out into the bright moonlight, and began to stroll up and down. Mark recognized many well-known figures. There was Honor, in white, walking with a little man who was conversing and gesticulating with considerable vivacity. She seemed preoccupied, and held her head high—gazing straight before her. Lookers on see most of the game. The man must be a dense idiot not to notice that she was not listening to one word he said.

There was Miss Paske, escorted by a ponderous companion with a rolling gait—Sir Gloster, of course—and Miss Lalla was undoubtedly entertaining him. It almost seemed as if he could hear his emphatic "excellent" where he stood. Mrs. Merryfeather and Captain Dorrington, Captain Merryfeather and Miss Fleet, and so on—and so on—as pair after pair came forth.

Suddenly he became aware of the fact that he was not the only spectator. Just below him stood a figure, so motionless, that he had taken it for part of a tree. The figure moved, and he saw the Persian lady standing gazing with fixed ravenous eyes on the scene below them. He made a slight movement, and she turned hastily and came up towards him. They were acquaintances of some standing now, and met once or twice a week either among the lepers or about the cantonment. Mark had never ventured to call at the mysterious little bungalow, but he sent her offerings of flowers, fruit, and hill partridges, and she in return admitted him to her friendship—to an entirely unprecedented extent. Whether this was due to the young man's handsome face, and chivalrous respect for her privacy and her sex, or whether it was accorded for the sake of another, who shall say?

"You are looking on, like myself," he remarked, as she accosted him. "Are you interested?"

"Nay, 'the world is drowned to him who is drowned,' says the proverb. I came to Hawal Bagh to retire from the crowd, and lo! a crowd is at my gates!"

"This, surely, must be quite a novel sight to you?"

She gazed at him questioningly, and made no answer.

"Of course you have never seen this sort of thing before, English people in evening dress, dancing to a band?"

"I have known phantoms—yea, I have seen such as these," pointing, "in a—dream—thousands of years ago."

Her companion made no reply, the Persian often uttered dark sayings that were totally beyond his comprehension. Possibly she believed in the transmigration of souls, and was alluding to a former existence.

"Mine are but spirits, whereas to you these people are real flesh and blood," she resumed. "You were one of them but three months ago. Think well ere you break with your past, and kill and bury youth. Lo, you grow old *already*! Let me plead for youth, and love. Heaven has opened to me to-day. She," lowering her voice to a whisper, "is among those—I have seen her—she is there below."

"I know," he answered, also in a low voice.

"Then why do you not seek her—so young, so fair, so good? Oh! have you forgotten her sweet smile, her charming eyes? Love, real love, comes but once! Go now and find her."

Mark shook his head with emphatic negation.

"What heart of stone!" she cried passionately. "Truly I will go myself and fetch her here. I——But no—I dare not," and she covered her face with her hands.

"Do not add your voice to my own mad inclinations. It is all over between us. To meet her and to part again would give her needless pain."

"Ah! again the music," murmured the Persian, as the band suddenly struck up a weird haunting waltz, which her companion well remembered—they had played it at the bachelors' ball. "Music," she continued, clenching her two hands, "of any kind has a sore effect on me. It tears my heart from my very body, and yet I love it, yea, though it transport me to——" She paused, unable to finish the sentence. Her lips trembled, her great dark eyes dilated, and she suddenly burst into a storm of tears. The sound of her wild, loud, despairing sobs, actually floated down and penetrated to the ears of a merry couple who were strolling at large, and now stood immediately below, little guessing that another pair on the hillside were sadly contemplating a scene of once familiar but now lost delights, like two poor wandering spirits.

"Surely," said Mrs. Merryfeather, "I heard a human voice, right up there above us. It sounded just like a woman weeping—crying as if her heart was broken."

"Oh, impossible!" scoffed the man. "Hearts in these days are warranted unbreakable, like toughened glass."

"Listen! There it is again!" interrupted the lady excitedly.

"Not a bit of it, my dear Mrs. Merry; and your sex would not feel flattered if they heard that you had mistaken the cry of a *wild beast*, for a woman's voice! I assure you, on my word of honour, that it is nothing but a hyena."

CHAPTER XLII.
BY THE OLD RIFLE-RANGE.

A powerful and determined temptation, that was deaf to reason or argument, struggled hourly to drag Mark Jervis to Hawal Bagh. It changed its fierce wrestlings, and passionate and even frantic pleadings to soft alluring whispers. It whispered that life was but an hour in the æons of time—a drop in the ocean of eternity. Why not taste the drop—enjoy the hour? Snatch the sunshine and live one's little day, ere passing for ever into eternal darkness and oblivion! It even quoted the Scriptures, and vehemently urged him to take no thought for the morrow—that sufficient unto the day was the evil thereof. It seized the brush from the hand of memory, and painted Honor Gordon as an angel. It babbled of a visit to Mrs. Brande—*she* had always been his friend. Surely there was no harm in going to see *her*! But the young man sternly silenced alike whisperings or pleadings. He beat the mad tempter to its knees, choked it, and, as he believed, put it to death. Why undergo the anguish of parting twice—why walk across red-hot plough-shares a second time?

For four whole days he held aloof, and never visited the cantonment—save in his thoughts and dreams. On the fifth he conscientiously set forth in the opposite direction, and after a long and aimless ride was astonished to find himself—no, not exactly on the enchanted ground, but close to the old rifle-range, which lay at the back of its encompassing hills. To the left dipped a long valley, on the right of the path towered a forest of rhododendrons and ever-green oaks, carpeted with ferns, and a blaze of delicate autumn flowers; here and there the Virginia creeper flared, and here and there a pale passion-flower had flung abroad its eager tendrils and attached two noble trees. All at once, a fat white puppy came bustling through the undergrowth; he was chasing a family of respectable elderly monkeys, with the audacity common to his age and race. Truly the pup is the father of the dog; and Jervis, who was walking slowly with his pony following him, recognized this particular pup at once as an old friend. He had bought him and presented him to Mrs. Brande, when her grief was as yet too fresh—and this same rollicking, well-to-do animal had once been indignantly spurned! To whom did he now belong? Who was his master or his mistress? There was a sound of light young footsteps, a crashing of small twigs, a glimpse of a white dress, and an anxious girlish voice calling, "Tommy, Tommy, Tommy!"

In another second Honor Gordon ran down into the path, about thirty yards ahead of Tommy's donor. She was almost breathless, her hat was in her hand—possibly it had been snatched off by an inquisitive branch as she struggled after the runaway. The soft little locks on her forehead were ruffled, and she had an unusually brilliant colour.

As Mark's starving eyes devoured her face he thought he had never seen her look so lovely. He summoned up all his self-command—there must be no going back to "old days," no moaning over "what might have been." No; he was the stronger, and must set a stern example.

For quite twenty seconds there was a dead silence, a silence only broken by the trickling of a snow-born mountain stream, passing lingeringly through the ferns and orchids—who seemed to stoop and bend over—listening intently to its timid silvery song.

"How changed he was!" thought Honor, with a queer tight feeling in her throat, "only three short months, and the bright look of buoyant youth had faded from his face."

"Ah!" she exclaimed, with a supreme effort. "I had a presentiment that I should see you soon—I dreamt it!"

"Dreams sometimes go by contraries," he answered, with a rather fixed smile.

"And how clever of Tommy to find you! The dear dog remembered you."

"Well, up to the present he has not shown any symptoms of recognizing me; on the contrary, he has cut me dead. He is in hot pursuit of some venerable lumgoors. How long is it since he has seen me?" asked Mark.

"The day of the bachelors' ball. I recollect you gave him a *méringue*, and very nearly killed him! It was on the eighth of June. This is the tenth of September; just three months and two days."

"So it is," he acquiesced, with forced *nonchalance*.

"Do you live near here?" she continued.

"About four miles, by a goat path across that hill."

"Pray are you aware that we are picnicing below, with half Shirani?"

"Yes, I know; but not another starvation picnic I hope?"

"And yet," ignoring his ill-timed jest, "you have never come to see us, and we leave to-morrow!"

He looked down to avoid her questioning eyes, and made no answer, beyond a faint, half-strangled sigh.

"At least we are still friends," she urged, swallowing something in her throat.

"Yes—always; but I thought I had better remain away. The Shirani folk would take me for a ghost, and I might upset their nerves. What is the latest station news?"

"Our latest news is, that Mrs. Sladen is to go home at Christmas. Miss Clover is engaged to Captain Burne, and Miss Paske to Sir Gloster Sandilands," she answered stiffly.

"Poor Toby! I suppose my former acquaintances believe me to be in England—if they ever think of me at all?"

She hesitated, twisted her ring round and round, and then said—

"Your friends," with emphasis, "know that you are out in this country, looking after your father. How is he?"

"Wonderfully better, thank you."

"And you—you have been ill?" she remarked rather tremulously.

"No, indeed; I never was better in my life. Of course you saw Waring before he went down?"

"No," with undeniable embarrassment. "In fact, he copied your example, and dispensed with all farewells. He—he—left rather suddenly," and she coloured.

"Why do you hesitate?" looking at her keenly. "What did he *do*? He has been doing something, I can see."

"It was rather what he did *not* do," with a constrained laugh. "Of course it is no business of mine. He did not pay any of his bills. I am not sure whether I ought to tell you."

"And I am quite sure you ought," he answered with decision.

"But he left such quantities of debts behind him, and no—address——"

"Debts?" he repeated incredulously.

"Yes, he paid for nothing. Club accounts, card accounts, mess bills, servants' wages—not even his bearer's bill for thread and buttons and blacking. People," with a nervous little laugh, "seem to think that was the greatest enormity of all!"

"No!" cried Mark, his pale face turning to a vivid red, "I will tell you of a greater. I knew he had spent and muddled away most of our joint-funds, and the day I was last in Shirani I collected the bills and gave him all the money I had in the world—a cheque for five hundred pounds—to settle our affairs.

He swore, on his honour, he would pay them at once and send me the receipts. Now, of course, every one in Shirani believes me to be as great a swindler and thief as he is! They must naturally suppose that I—I—bolted from my creditors! I," with increasing warmth, "now understand why you stammered and hesitated when I asked if I was not forgotten. Forgotten! I shall live in people's memories for years—on the principle that 'the evil which men do lives after them.'"

"I am sorry I told you——" she began eagerly.

"And I have chiefly myself to blame. I was an idiot to trust Waring. I had had one lesson; but—I was half mad with my own troubles, and determined to tear myself away from Shirani at once. I felt that if I stayed on I might yield to temptation—good resolutions and fresh impressions might fade—and I might never return here——"

The pup, flouted and evaded by the scornful lumgoors, and exhausted by his tremendous efforts, now squatted on the path, apparently listening open-mouthed to every word.

The grey pony had also drawn near, and occasionally rubbed his handsome head against his master's shoulder, as much as to say—"Enough of such fooling; let us move on!"

"This is horrible!" continued Mark. "I hate to owe a penny, and I have no means of paying our joint-debts, for Waring has wolfed the cheque."

"And your uncle?"

"He has never written once. From his point of view I have treated him atrociously, and I am awfully sorry he should think so, for I am very fond of him. Of course he has done with me." And, with a grim smile, "I am now in sober truth—a *real* poor relation. I am a pretty sort of fellow," he went on, "I have talked of nothing but myself—and money—money—money, for the last five minutes. Tell me of *yourself*. Are you having a good time?"

"*A good time?*" she echoed, with a flash of her dark grey eyes.

"I beg your pardon, Honor," he said, humbly. "But it has been one of my few consolations when I roam about these hills, to think that you were happier than I am."

"And had forgotten *you*?" she added expressively.

"And," with a slight tremor in his voice—"had forgotten *me*."

"Never!" she returned, with passionate energy.

"Yes—you will, in time; perhaps not for two or three years—for you are not like other girls. I am your first lover—nothing can deprive me of that memory."

"No, nothing," she admitted, almost in a whisper.

"But, you know, they say a woman generally marries her *second* love," with a laborious effort to speak steadily.

"How calmly you can discuss my lovers, and my future!" cried Honor, indignantly. "Oh, how hard you have become—how cold—how cruel!"

"Cruel—if I am cruel—only to be kind," he replied steadily. "For, years to come, you will thank me—and think——"

"I think," she interrupted, with a pitiful little gesture, "that when we meet so—seldom—scarcely ever—that you might be——" here her voice totally failed her.

She had grown much paler, and her breath came quickly, as she tried to keep down a sob.

Mark resisted a wild impulse to take her in his arms—and stooping, picked up the pup instead.

"Your uncle got my letter?" he asked, in a cool formal tone.

"Yes, and was dreadfully concerned; but he said you were a man of honour, and your views and his were identical—but—I don't agree with them."

"You don't agree with them! What do you mean?"

"He told auntie, of course—and of course I insisted on her telling *me*. After all, it was my affair. I know the obstacle—I am ready to be your wife, just the same. As for poverty——"

"Poverty," he interrupted quickly, "is not the question! I have a little money of my own, and I could put my shoulder to the wheel and work for you, Honor. It is not that—it is that my future is overshadowed, my reason stalked, by an hereditary and implacable enemy. I have no right to drag another into the pit—and, please God, I never will! When I lived a smooth luxurious sort of life, in those days that seem years ago, I thirsted for some difficult task, something to do that would single me out and set me apart from other men. My task has been allotted to me; it is not what I desired——"

"No!" interposed Honor, whose heart was fighting against her fate with a frenzy of despair. "Your task is to renounce everything—the world, and friends, and wealth, and *me*—and to bury yourself in these remote hills, with a crazy old gentleman who cannot realize the sacrifice. Don't!" with an impatient gesture of her hand, "I know that *I* am speaking as if *I* were mad, and in my old foolish way. I know in my heart that you are doing what is right—that you could not do otherwise, and I—I am proud of you."

Then, as she looked into his haggard, altered face and miserable eyes, and caught a glimpse of the real Mark beneath his armour of stoicism—"But, oh, it is hard—it is hard——" she added, as she covered her face with her hands and wept.

"Honor! for God's sake don't—don't—I implore you! I cannot bear this. I would go through all I have struggled with over again to save you one tear. Circumstances—destiny—or whatever they call it—is too strong for us. You must not let me spoil your life. You know I shall love you—you only as long as I draw breath."

"I know that!" raising her wet eyes to his. "And you *dare* to talk to me of a good time, of marrying my second love! Oh, Mark, Mark! how could you?"

"I was a brute to say it. I thought it would make it easier for you—when——" and his voice broke—"sometimes—when—you think of me——"

"Which will be every day—and often. And now I must be going. I was already late enough when Tommy ran away. I was afraid of his meeting poor Ben's fate. Will you come with me as far as the brow of the hill, where our paths part?"

"Yes—part for ever!" he added to himself.

As they turned, she asked him many questions concerning his life, his associates, and his occupations. He on his side made the best of everything, painting the Yellow Bungalow, the gardens, the planters and missionaries with gorgeous colours.

"And are there no white women near you?" she inquired. "Have you never met one lady to speak to since you left Shirani?"

"Yes, I have one acquaintance, and one who is a friend of yours. She is a Persian, I believe. Your little cornelian ring has been a strong link between us. She is a most mysterious person. No one can tell who she is, or where she came from. All we know is, that she spends her present time in doing good, nursing the sick and dying. She told me that you knew the history of her life—you alone——"

"It is true," bending her head as she spoke, and fixing her eyes on the ground.

"She shrinks from all observation, but she does not hide from *me*—for your sake; we talk about you constantly, I may say always."

"Then give her a message from me, please. Tell her that I often think of her, and ask her if I may write to her, or if she will write to me?"

"You forget that she is a Persian. How can she possibly write to you?"

Honor coloured painfully, and twisted her ring round and round before she spoke, and then she said—

"Please give her the message all the same. I—I—can manage to get her letter read. *I* will understand it."

They were now at the point where their roads diverged—his went along the hill, hers led down into the valley. She stopped for a moment, and caressed the grey pony's sleek hard neck; then she turned and gave the pony's master both her hands. They gazed at one another, with sad white faces, reading their life's tragedy in each other's eyes. Then she suddenly tore her fingers from his clasp, and ran down the hill with Tommy in pursuit. Jervis stood where she had left him, until the very last echo of her footsteps had died away.

"And that is a sound I shall *never* hear again," he groaned aloud, and flinging himself down on the root of a tree, he covered his face with his hands. How long he remained in this attitude the grey pony alone knew! By-and-by he became tired of waiting—for he was either too well fed or too sympathetic to graze—he came and rubbed his soft black muzzle against the man's short brown locks (his cap lay on the ground). It was his poor little attempt at consolation, and effectually roused his owner, though it did not comfort him, for what could a dumb animal know of the great distresses of the human heart?

Honor was late for tiffin, in fact it was getting on for afternoon teatime when she arrived. She discovered the bungalow in a state of unusual commotion. There was visible excitement on the servants' faces, an air of extra importance (were that possible) in the bearer's barefooted strut—he now appeared to walk almost entirely on his heels.

Mrs. Brande was seated at a writing-table, beginning and tearing up dozens of notes; her cap was askew, her fair hair was ruffled, and her face deeply flushed. What could have happened?

"Oh, Honor, my child, I thought you were never coming back, I have been longing for you," rushing at her. "But how white you look, dearie; you have walked too far. Are you ill?"

"No, no, auntie. What is it? There is something in the air. What has happened?"

For sole answer, Mrs. Brande cast her unexpected weight upon her niece's frail shoulder, and burst into loud hysterical tears.

"Only think, dear girl!"—convulsive sobs—"a coolie has just come—and brought a letter from P.—They have made him a K.C.B."—boisterous sobs—"and your poor old auntie—is—*a lady at last*!"

CHAPTER XLIII.
"RAFFLE IT!"

"Major and Mrs. Granby Langrishe request the honour of Mr. and Mrs. Blanks's company at St. John's church at two o'clock on the afternoon of the 20th inst., to be present at the marriage of their niece and Sir Gloster Sandilands."

These invitation cards, richly embossed in silver, were to be seen in almost every abode in Shirani. The wedding dress was on its way from Madame Phelps, in Calcutta. The cake and champagne were actually in the house. There were to be no bridesmaids, only two little pages—"they were cheaper," Mrs. Langrishe said to herself; "a set of girls would be expecting jewellery and bouquets." Happy Mrs. Langrishe, who had been overwhelmed with letters and telegrams of congratulations. She had indeed proved herself to be *the* clever woman of the family. It was her triumph—more than Lalla's—and she was radiant with pride and satisfaction. Yea, her self-congratulations were fervent. She was counting the days until her atrocious little incubus went down the ghaut as Lady Sandilands. A little incubus, securely fastened on another person's shoulders—for life!

Lalla was entirely occupied with letters, trousseau, and preparations. She was to have taken the principal part in a grand burlesque, written specially for her, by Toby Joy. The burlesque had been on hand for two months, and was to bring the Shirani season to a fitting and appropriate close. The piece was called "Sinbad the Sailor." Lalla had been rehearsing her songs and dances most industriously, until she had been called upon to play another part—the part of Sir Gloster's *fiancée*.

Sir Gloster did not care for burlesques; he had never seen Miss Paske in her true element—never seen her dance. It was not befitting her future position that she should appear on the boards. No, no; he assured her that he was somewhat old-fashioned, his mother would not like it. She must promise him to relinquish the idea, and never to perform in public again. But Lalla was stubborn; she would not yield altogether. Urged by Toby Joy, by the theatrical troupe—who felt that they could not pull through without their own bright particular star—she held out in a most unreasonable and astonishing manner. At length she submitted so far as to declare that "she would wear Turkish trousers, if he liked!" This she reluctantly announced, as if making an enormous concession.

"He certainly did *not* wish her to wear Turkish trousers!" he returned, greatly scandalized. "*How* could she make such a terrible suggestion?" He was heavy and inert, but he could oppose a dead, leaden weight of resistance to any scheme which he disliked. This *he* called "manly determination;" but Lalla had another name for it—"pig-headed obstinacy!" However, she coaxed, promised, flattered, wept, and worked upon her infatuated lover so successfully, that he reluctantly permitted her to take a very small part, so as not to have her name removed from the bills; but this was to be positively "Her last appearance," and she might announce it on the placards, if she so pleased. He himself was summoned to Allahabad on urgent business—in fact, to arrange about settlements—and he would not be present, he feared; but he would do his best to return by the end of the week.

Miss Paske's part, the dancing, singing peri, was given to a very inferior performer—who was the stage manager's despair, and a most hopeless stick. Freddy Joy, who was in woefully low spirits respecting the certain failure of the burlesque, and—other matters—came to Lalla on the night but one before the play.

"She has got influenza—so it's all *up*," making a feint of tearing his hair, "and every place in the house sold for two nights, and—an awful bill for dresses and properties. What is to become of me? Can't you take it? It was your own part—you do it splendidly—no professional could beat you. Come, Lalla!"

"I promised I would not dance," she answered with a solemn face.

"Time enough to tie yourself up with promises after you are married! Take your fling *now*—you have only ten days—you'll never dance again."

"No, never," she groaned.

"He is away, too," urged this wicked youth; "he is not coming up till Saturday; he won't know, till all is over, and then he will be as proud as a peacock. You have your dresses, you had everything ready until he came and spoilt the whole 'box of tricks.'" And Toby looked unutterable things. "Did he say anything to your aunt?" he asked.

"No—not a word. You don't suppose that I allow *her* to mix herself up in my affairs? It was merely between him and me——"

"Well, you can easily smooth him down—and if you don't take your own original part, I must send round a peon this afternoon, to say that the burlesque has been put off, owing to the illness of the prima-donna—the 'incapability' is the proper word. But you are a brick, and you won't let it come to *that*; you will never leave us in a hole."

A little dancing devil in each eye eagerly assured him that she would not fail them! Yes, the combined entreaties of her own set—their compliments and flattery—her own hungry craving for what Toby called "one last fling," carried the point. *He* would not be back until Saturday. The piece was for Wednesday, Thursday, and Friday, and she could (as she believed) easily talk him over. Yes, she made up her mind that she would play the peri; and she informed her aunt, with her most off-hand air, "that she had been prevailed on to take the principal part; that Miss Lane was ill (and any way would have been a dead failure); that she could not be so shamefully *selfish* as to disappoint every one; that the proceeds were for a charity (after the bills were paid there would not be much margin)", and Mrs. Langrishe, in sublime ignorance of Lalla's promise, acquiesced as usual. She now subscribed to all her niece's suggestions with surprising amiability, assuring herself that the days of her deliverance from "a girl in a thousand" were close at hand!

The burlesque of Sinbad was beautifully staged, capitally acted, and a complete success. Miss Paske's dancing and singing were pronounced to be worthy of a London theatre—if not of a music-hall. People discussed her wherever they met, and all the men hastened, as it were in a body, to book places for the next performance.

The ladies were not altogether so enthusiastic; indeed, some of them were heard to wonder how Sir Gloster would have liked it?

Sir Gloster, on the wings of love, was already half way through his return journey. He had transacted his business with unexpected promptitude, and was breakfasting at a certain dâk bungalow, encompassed with many parcels and boxes. Here he was joined by two subalterns, who were hurrying in the opposite direction—that is, from Shirani to the plains. They were full of the last evening's entertainment, and could talk of nothing but the burlesque.

"It was quite A1," they assured their fellow-traveller. "It could not be beaten in London—no, not even at the Empire. Miss Paske was simply ripping!"

"Yes," returned Sir Gloster, complacently, "I believe there is a good deal of nice feeling in her acting, but she had only a minor part."

"Bless your simple, innocent heart!" exclaimed the other, "she was the principal figure; she was the whole show; she filled the bill."

"May I ask what you mean?" demanded the baronet, with solemn white dignity.

"She was the peri—didn't you *know*? She dances every bit as well as Lottie Collins or Sylvia Grey, doesn't she, Capel?" appealing eagerly to his comrade.

"Yes; and I'd have gone to see her again to-night, only for this beastly court-martial. I gave my ticket over to Manders, for he couldn't get a place. She draws like a chimney on fire; there is no squeezing in at the door—even window-sills were at a premium. You ought to go on, Sir Gloster; of course *you* will get a seat," with a significant laugh. "This is the last performance, and, upon my word, you should not *miss* it."

Sir Gloster remained mute. Was it possible that his little Lalla, who wrote him such sweet, endearing notes, had deliberately broken her word, and defied him?

At the very thought of such a crime his white flabby face grew rigid. Seeing was believing. He would take this crack-brained young man's advice, and hurry on. He might manage to be in Shirani by eight o'clock that evening—just in time to dress and get to the play.

His wrath was hot within him—and the anger of a quiet and lethargic person, when once roused, is a very deadly thing. His sturdy hill ponies bore the first brunt of his indignation; and Sir Gloster, who was naturally a timid horseman, for once threw fear to the winds, and galloped as recklessly as Toby Joy himself. He arrived at the club just in time to swallow a few mouthfuls, change his clothes, and set off to the theatre. He could not get a seat, but "he might, if he liked, stand near the door, with his back to the wall," and for this handsome privilege he paid four rupees—the best-laid-out money he ever invested, as he subsequently declared. The curtain had already risen; the scene looked marvellously like fairyland. Toby Joy had just concluded a capital topical song, when a large egg was carefully rolled upon the stage. The egg-shell opened without the application of a spoon, and hatched out a most exquisite creature, the peri, whose appearance was the signal for a thunder of hand-clapping. The peri—yes—was Lalla, in very short, fleecy petticoats, with a twinkling star in her hair—his own present, as Sir Gloster noted with an additional spasm of indignation.

Presently she began to dance.

Now, be it known, that her performance was perfectly decorous and delightfully graceful. Lalla's glancing feet scarcely touched the ground, and she danced as if from pure happiness and lightness of heart. (Toby Joy danced as if he had *le diable au corps*.) After entrancing the spectators for ten thrilling minutes with several entirely fresh variations, Lalla finished up with the tee-to-tum spin, which is to the dancer what the high note, at the end of a song, is to the singer!

The result of this effort was a hurricane of frantic applause, in which Sir Gloster took no part; he was not a theatre-goer—he was provincial. His mother and his surroundings were strictly evangelical; and whilst his *fiancée* enchanted the whole station, he stood against the wall glowering and pale. The only character present to his mind was *the daughter of Herodias*! Frankly speaking, the performance had filled him with horror. That the future Lady Sandilands should offer herself thus to public contemplation; that any one who chose to pay four rupees might see this indecorous exhibition—including soldiers in uniform, at the low price of four annas!

He was actually beside himself with fury, and forced his way out, with his head down, like a charging animal. Few noticed him or his hasty exit; every one had eyes for Lalla, and Lalla only. She received an ovation and a shower of bouquets as she was conducted before the curtain by Toby Joy, modestly curtseying and kissing her hand. Miss Paske subsequently remained to enjoy a merry and *recherché* supper, chaperoned by the invaluable Mrs. Dashwood; and Mrs. Langrishe, as was not an unusual occurrence, went home alone.

To that lady's great amazement, she discovered Sir Gloster awaiting her in the drawing-room, and she gathered from his strange and agitated appearance that something terrible had occurred.

"I was thinking of writing to you, Mrs. Langrishe," he began in a curiously formal voice, "but I changed my mind, and came to see you instead. All is over between your niece and myself."

Mrs. Langrishe turned perfectly livid, and dropped into the nearest chair.

"Pray, explain!" she faltered at last.

"Miss Paske will doubtless *explain* to you why she gave me a solemn promise to renounce dancing on a public stage. I reluctantly allowed her to appear for the last time in a very small part—that of an old nurse. I return unexpectedly, and discover her in the character of a ballet-girl, exhibiting herself—well, I must say it—half naked to the whole of Shirani. Such a person is not fit to be my wife. She has broken her word. She has a depraved taste; she has no modesty."

That Ida Langrishe should live to hear such epithets applied to her own flesh and blood!

She covered her face with her hands, and actually sobbed aloud. Who had ever seen Mrs. Langrishe break down before? No one.

"Oh, dear Sir Gloster," she began hysterically (she would need all her fascinations now), "Lalla is so young" (only twenty-six). "She is easily worked upon, she is in great request; the burlesque would have fallen through—and it is for *such* a good charity—if she had not, at the eleventh hour, consented to take a part."

"I cannot accept your excuses, my dear madam" (waving both fat hands, like the flappers of an angry seal). "I could never trust Miss Paske again. Imagine the future Lady Sandilands, displaying her arms—and, excuse me, her legs—in ungraceful antics for the amusement of any one who chose to pay two or three rupees. At the eleventh hour, I absolutely refuse to marry her!"

"You are not afraid of a breach of promise case?" asked Mrs. Langrishe in despair. She was indeed dying in the last ditch.

"Not in the least," was the bold reply. "No man—no gentleman is compelled to marry an amateur mountebank! Oh, if my poor dear mother had been present this night, I believe the shock would have killed her! However, I am grateful for small mercies; I am thankful that I saw Miss Paske in her true colours, before it was too late!"

"The invitations are out days ago; the trousseau is almost complete; the presents have come in shoals; the cake is actually in the house,—what *am* I to do?" pleaded unhappy Mrs. Langrishe, in a transport of anguish.

"I'm sure I don't know. I wash my hands of the whole affair. I am going down to-morrow morning."

"To-morrow morning!" repeated the unfortunate lady.

"Yes, I have no personal ill-will or ill-feeling against *you*, Mrs. Langrishe," he continued, as if he were offering her some superb token of generosity. "It is not your fault, though I must confess that I always thought you rather spoiled Miss Paske. However, in the present instance, I hold you entirely blameless; but *noblesse oblige*—and I—a—really could not ask my mother, and friends, to receive a young a—a—lady—whose proper sphere is pantomime and—all that sort of thing!" And waving his adieux, with a large tremulous hand, he stalked out, and with him Mrs. Langrishe saw depart Lalla's brilliant prospects, her own reputation as a clever woman, and the solid embodiment of an immense outlay of forbearance—flattery—and rupees.

She sat for a long time over the dying wood fire, her face the colour of its ashes.

At three o'clock in the morning Lalla (a true rake at heart) had not returned, and her impending interview was thus postponed for twelve hours. It was past three o'clock in the afternoon when Miss Paske sauntered into her aunt's room. Mrs. Langrishe was prostrate, from the double effect of a sleepless night and a nervous headache.

Lalla listened to her outburst incredulously. She had dressed herself with special care, collected all her bouquets, and had resolved to enact a pretty little semi-penitential scene, with her stolid, easy-going, somewhat dull *fiancé*. She expected him now at any moment. What was this her aunt was saying? He had come; and seen; and fled! Impossible! He had been present last night! For once, she signally failed to sneer down, laugh down, or in any way suppress or silence her relative. Oh! she had been *mad* to listen to Toby Joy, she was always too ready to be over-persuaded by him. He had had nothing on the hazard, whilst she had her all at stake. And her magnificent prospects, her title, her diamonds, were at that moment rapidly rumbling down hill in the rickety mail tonga.

The presents, the invitations, the breakfast—what people would say, especially her own people, and the not unnatural elation of old Mother Brande, on whom she had ruthlessly trampled—all these things flashed through her mind.

She would, of *course*, be sent home immediately. What a horrible outlook. To remain till the end of her days, as a sort of "object lesson," a terrible living example, in the corner of her father's large shabby country house. She would be pointed out to her younger sisters, and to others, as the old maid who had had her chance, and had danced it away!

During all this time her aunt was speaking fluently, ceaselessly, passionately, but to deaf ears—for Lalla was listening to her own thoughts, and too much occupied by the clamour of an inward voice to heed these outpourings.

At last one sentence struck her ear.

"And what is to be done with the cake, that has cost two hundred rupees, and is now in my storeroom?" demanded Mrs. Langrishe, dramatically.

"Raffle it," cried Lalla, with a reckless laugh, "or have another starvation picnic, and give them wedding-cake and sugar ornaments!"

"*Lalla!*" shrieked her aunt, in a voice that would have sounded strange even to her most intimate friends. "You are the most abominable, unprincipled, devilish——"

"Oh, don't bother!" interrupted Lalla, savagely; and she went out of the room, and gave the door a bang that caused the very cheval-glass to stagger in its place.

Once in her own bower, Lalla turned the key and flung herself into an armchair, knocking, as she did so, a parcel off a table at her elbow. She stooped and picked it up mechanically. It was a birthday-book, one of her numerous wedding presents, and had arrived that morning. She opened it in order to search for the verse opposite the date of the day. Perhaps it would give her a clue as to her future plans. For Lalla was extremely superstitious, and often shaped her course by means of the most trivial instruments, which were accepted by her as signs, tokens, and omens. Idiotic and preposterous as it may appear, she attributed all her present misfortune, not to her own deceit and folly—oh dear, no!—but to the disastrous fact of having had a *green* dress in her trousseau, and that was entirely Aunt Ida's doing, no fault of hers.

Yes, Lalla had a curious temperament, and an imagination open to every fantastic influence. As she whirled over the leaves of the book, she said to herself, "I will take this as final, and abide by it, for bad or good."

It was the eleventh of September, and the lines were—

"Retired from all, reserved, and coy,

To musing prone alone."

SCOTT.

"What utter bosh!" she exclaimed, passionately; then, like all dissatisfied inquirers, she determined to cast her first resolve to the winds and have yet another experiment—one more dip into the lottery of Fate.

"I'll see what it says for the twentieth—my wedding day, that was to have been——"

She turned to the page, and the lines were—

"He has not a shilling, nor has he a care."

ANON.

"There, that settles it," cried Lalla, tossing the hook down and moving quickly to her writing-table.

In a few hours the news of the ruptured alliance was all over Shirani. Another piece of intelligence was faintly whispered, but not credited, for it was really *too* much for the gossip-mongers to digest all at once. This last item declared "that Miss Paske and Mr. Joy had been seen flying down the cart road in a special tonga. They had run away—she, from her aunt's reproaches, and he, from his regimental duty. They were both absent without leave."

For once rumour proved to be true in every particular. The pair were married at the first church they came to, and subsequently joined an English theatrical company that were touring in India, and accompanied them to the Straits Settlements, China, and Japan.

Toby and Lalla act under the professional alias of "Mr. and Mrs. Langrishe," to the unspeakable indignation of the rightful owners of the name.

Lalla had written her aunt a most wicked, flippant, impertinent, heartless, in fact, diabolical letter, mentioning that the name of Langrishe would now be surrounded by distinction and a lustre of fame,—and for the first time.

It was many months before the stately Ida recovered her mental equilibrium, and her spirits. The experiences she had undergone at the hands of "a girl in a thousand" had aged her considerably; there are now a good many lines in her smooth, ivory-tinted face, and silver threads among her well-dressed brown locks.

Every one tacitly avoids the subject of broken-off engagements, theatricals, and nieces in her presence; and it would be a truly bold woman (such as is *not* Mrs. Brande) who would venture to inquire "what had become of her charming niece, who *was* to have married the baronet?"

CHAPTER XLIV.
A ROSE—CARRIAGE PAID.

"Sahib, there is some one coming—in a jampan," was the bearer's surprising announcement to Jervis, who was sitting under a tree in the garden, busily engaged in painting a portrait of the bearer's grandson. Now, a jampan, or dandy, is a sort of hill sedan-chair, and a mode of conveyance exclusively reserved for ladies.

Who could the lady be who was coming to the Pela Kothi? thought the young man, starting to his feet. Honor? Impossible! Mrs. Brande? No—the big picnic had dispersed ten days ago. He hurried out into the verandah, and shaded his eyes with his hand. Yes, sure enough, a dandy, borne by four men, and containing some one holding an enormous white umbrella—some one being carried backwards up the hill, followed by a native on a pony and two coolies with luggage. The *cortége* were distinctly making for the house, for they turned off the road into the direct path; but all that was visible was the white umbrella bobbing along among the tall jungle grass—and the white umbrella was approaching, as sure as fate.

For the last week Mark had noticed a great change in his father. As his mind strengthened, his bodily health appeared to fail—the hundred turns on the terrace were gradually lessening each morning as the steps that paced them became feebler and feebler, and the daily routine was now entirely set aside. An early ride had been Mark's chief relaxation, then breakfast with his father, afterwards he read the paper to him, talked to him, walked with him, until about three o'clock, when Major Jervis went to sleep—and slept almost uninterruptedly till dinner time. Meanwhile his son walked over to see one of the neighbours, or sketched—he had made quite a gallery of types and portraits—or took his gun to try his luck among the hills.

The major was always at his best in the evening. He enjoyed a game of chess, picquet, or *écarté*; and he liked to talk of his experiences, his old friends and comrades, to smoke, to tell the same long stories over and over again, and it was often one or two o'clock in the morning ere his son could prevail on him to extinguish his hookah and go to bed. But for the last week or ten days there had been no late hours, and no strolling round the garden, or basking in the sun, and Mark had never left the place. He feared that his father was about to have some kind of an attack—whether bodily or mental, he was too inexperienced to say—and he had despatched a note that very morning to Mr. Burgess, asking him to ride over and see his patient.

Meanwhile the visitor was coming steadily nearer and nearer, the umbrella effectually concealing his or her identity. In due time the dandy was carried up backwards into the verandah, turned right-about-face, and set down. And behold—under the umbrella sat—Mr. Pollitt!

Mr. Pollitt, looking exceedingly pleased with himself, and wearing a neat tweed Norfolk jacket, a courier bag, and an Elwood helmet. In one hand he clutched the umbrella, in the other an Indian Bradshaw.

"Uncle Dan!" almost shouted his nephew.

"There, my boy! Now, now, don't drag me—don't drag me. Let me get out; give me time. I," as he stood beside his nephew, "thought I would take you by surprise." And he shook his hand vigorously.

"A surprise—I should just think so! How on earth did you ever find your way here? Why did you not write?"

"I'll tell you everything presently—meanwhile, get me something to drink. I don't want lunch—get me a drink; and then walk me about like a horse, for my legs are so stiff with sitting in that infernal chair, that I believe I have lost the use of them."

As Mr. Pollitt drank off a whisky and soda, his little eyes wandered round the big dining-room with its faded magnificence, then strayed to the matchless prospect from the open window, and finally rested on his companion.

"Hullo, Mark, my boy! I see that this country has not agreed with you."

"Well, apparently it suits you, Uncle Dan," was the smiling reply. "You are looking very fit at any rate."

"And how is your father?"

"Rather shaky, I am afraid; he has been ailing for the last week. He is asleep just now."

"Ah, very well, then you can explain *me* to him when he awakes; and, meanwhile, I have a good many things to explain to *you*—why I am here, for instance. So, take me outside, where I can stretch my legs. There seems to be a great garden hereabouts.

"And now, to begin my story at the beginning," continued Mr. Pollitt, as they paced along side by side, "I got your letter, of course—and of course it upset me terribly. I was like a lunatic, and it did not smooth me down when some one kept saying, 'I told you so; still waters run deep!' and so on. At first I was resolved to cut you adrift, and to take no further notice of you. I was in this mind for a whole fortnight, and then I got another communication that drove me stark mad. I heard through my bankers that you had drawn on me for five thousand pounds. Now you know, Mark," coming to a full stop and holding up a finger, "I have never grudged you money, have I? but to take it like this. Don't interrupt me. I had given Bostock and Bell a quiet notification that I would honour your cheques to an additional small extent, in case, I thought to myself, the boy runs short of a couple of hundred or so—but five thousand! Yes, yes; I know you never had it! Don't *interrupt*, I tell you; let me go straight on. I wrote out to Bombay at once, asking for particulars, and the answer came back, 'That Mr. Jervis had drawn the money personally, in notes and gold, and had sailed for Australia—with a *lady*.'"

"Sailed for Australia with a *lady*!" repeated Mark, now halting in his turn on the gravel walk.

"Yes. At first I thought that I saw the whole thing as clear as print. Your letter was a ruse to gain time. You knew I was dead against your engagement to Miss Gordon, that I wanted you to come home, so you had just taken the matter into your own hands, helped yourself to what would start you fairly well, married the girl, and emigrated to the colonies. I kept this idea to myself, I am now most thankful to say, and I worried and worried over the business night and day. The whole affair was unlike you; but it was not very unlike Clarence. And where was Clarence? I thought of writing and making more inquiries—indeed, the sheet of paper was actually before me—when I suddenly said, 'Why should not I go out myself, instead of twopence-half-penny worth of paper?' Mrs. Pollitt was away at Homburg, I was alone, and, to tell you the truth, had no heart for shooting or anything. To put the matter in a nutshell, instead of writing, I went straight off to the P. and O. office and booked my passage to Bombay by the following mail. I thought I would just go out quietly and see for myself how the land lay. I came out the end of August. Phew! I feel hot now, when I think of those days in the Red Sea—a blazing sun, an iron steamer. I was like a lobster in a fish-kettle! Needless to say, there were no lords or dukes on board; but I travelled with what suited me *better*—an uncommonly clever lawyer chap, who lives in Bombay, and put me up to everything. We became great cronies, and as we smoked together a good bit, I told him the whole of my affairs, and placed myself unreservedly in his hands; and for once in my life I did a wise thing. He wanted me to stay with him, but I put up at an hotel. However, he rigged me out, engaged a first class Goanese servant for me, who speaks English, and takes me entirely in charge, just as if I was a baby, and he set about ferreting out the cheque business. I saw the cheque—it was your signature sure enough; but the writing of 'five thousand pounds' was another hand—Clarence's. I discovered that he had passed off as you. His photograph was identified at the bank. I could not hear anything about the lady; but she was entered in the passenger list for Melbourne as 'Mrs. Jervis.' So exit Waring—and a nice child's guide *he* has proved!"

"That is not all," burst out Mark. "He owes money all over the place! I gave him the command of all our funds, and he squandered every penny."

"Serve you jolly well right," returned his uncle with emphasis.

"Yes; it certainly did. I also gave him a cheque for five hundred to pay off everything the day I left Shirani. I was so bothered, that I conclude that I never filled in the cheque properly."

"Evidently not, and your little oversight cost me four thousand five hundred pounds. Well, never mind that now. I heard pretty stories of Clarence at the hotel—people talking at the table beside me; how he had gambled, betted, and played the deuce, and made a regular cat's-paw of the young fool he was travelling with, meaning *you*—an undeniable fact. I then, having finished off Waring, came straight away to look you up, Master Mark. Pedro, that's my fellow, took great care of me, and I have had as many adventures as would fill a volume of *Punch*. I travelled in comfort as long as I was on the rail, bar the heat; but once the rail came to an end, and I had to take to a box—I am too old to begin riding—I was uncommonly sorry for myself. However, everything I saw was new and interesting, the scenery splendid; I came *viâ* Shirani, of course, and I broke my journey at the Brandes—Sir Pelham and Lady Brande. By the way, you never told me that he had a handle to his name! Eh, how was that?"

"And how came you to know the Brandes?" asked his nephew gravely.

"Ah, that is another story! And how came *you* to tell Sir Pelham that there was insanity in the Jervis family, eh?"

"Because it is true. And I only heard it since I came here. My grandfather died in Richmond lunatic asylum, my uncle jumped overboard at sea, my father has now, thank God, a lucid interval, but he has been insane for years."

"Lies, every one of them!" blazed out Mr. Pollitt.

"Uncle Dan, what do you mean?" demanded Jervis, with trembling lips and a pair of sternly searching eyes.

"I know the Jervis family; why, man, I made it my business to study it up. Your grandfather, a splendid old soldier, died at Richmond in his own house, as sane as I am—saner, indeed, for I've been near losing my senses several times of late. Your uncle, noble fellow, jumped overboard to save life and lost his own. Your father's head was cracked by a fall. Who told you this other balderdash?"

"Fernandez, my father's heir. He was informed by Mrs. Jervis, my late stepmother. And it is all true what you tell me?"

"As true as I am a living man and sinner. Your father, no doubt, believed every one of his people to be lunatics, a phase of his own delusions."

"Uncle Dan," broke in his nephew, "I don't think you can ever realize what you have done for me. You have restored me—to life—to hope. That was the reason why I gave up Miss Gordon."

"And she is staunch to you still," nodding his head emphatically.

"How on earth do you know?"

"Oh, I know a good deal, considering that I have only been a fortnight in the country! Mark, my dear boy, I see that all this sudden news is too much for you."

"Go on—go on," cried the other, white with excitement; "such news is never too much for any one."

"Well, you know, I came up by that maddening, twisting cart road—I began to think it had no ending, like eternity. You recollect the fountains, every few miles? At one of them, my fellows stopped to drink and smoke, and there was a lady watering her horse—a remarkably handsome girl, riding a fine black Arab. She had a white puppy on her knee. She looked so pleasant, that though, as you know, I'm a shy man, I ventured to speak to her, and asked her if the road led to any place, short of China? or if she had ever *heard* of Shirani? Yes, she lived there; and it was just four miles further. We fell into talk, we were going the same way—her horse would not stand the puppy at any price, but reared, and flung about like a mad thing. She sat him splendidly, I will say, and held on to the dog like grim death; she said he was tired—and the long and the short of it was, that *I* took the pup in the dandy, and of all the nasty fidgeting little brutes!—but that girl has such beautiful eyes—I could do anything for her. And I'd like to see the man that could resist her! I told her my name, and said I had come out after my nephew, and asked her if she had ever heard of him—his name was Jervis. She immediately became bright scarlet, I do assure you, and said 'Yes.' I ventured to inquire her name. She said it was Gordon; and when I replied, 'I have heard of *you*,' she grew, if possible, still redder. We became as thick as thieves in no time. I got out and walked beside her, actually carrying the pup—for he would not sit in the dandy alone—and she told me a lot about the hill folk, and the mountain peaks, and taught me a few words of Hindostani. I inquired about an hotel, and she declared that there was none, and I must come to her uncle's; he and her aunt would be very glad to see me, for Mr. Jervis was a particular friend of theirs. And is he not a particular friend of *yours* too? I asked as pointedly as I knew how. And she looked me straight in the face, and said '*Yes.*' I stayed with the Brandes, to make a long story short, and I was delighted with my visit. I now know what people mean when they talk of Indian hospitality and Indian friends. I believe I am getting quite attached to the country!"

"Then you had better remain out here, Uncle Dan, and live with me."

"A case of Mahomet and the mountain, eh? No, no, my boy; I mean to fetch you home. I cannot spare you. At my age it is impossible to throw out new roots."

"And about Miss Gordon?" urged his listener impatiently.

"Honor, you mean. She was charming. She may have wished to turn my poor silly old head, and she succeeded. She played the violin—*that* settled me. Yesterday morning, before I left, she and I were walking in the garden quite early, and she picked me a button-hole; and I said, 'I'm off now to see my boy. Will you give me a flower for him, and have you any message?' She made no answer for a full minute; so, to put her at ease, I said, 'I know all about it, my dear. I was angry to think that he could leave me; but what was that to leaving *you*!' 'He did what was right,' she said, firing up like a sky-rocket. When we had made peace again, she chose a flower with most particular care, and said with a face as red as the rose, 'You may give him that, with my love.' 'Certainly,' I said; 'but the carriage must be prepaid.' At first she did not understand."

"And I must confess that I am equally at sea," admitted his companion.

"Why, you young donkey, of course I made her give me a kiss."

"Which is more than she has ever given me. Uncle Dan, you are an extraordinarily able man. No wonder you made a great fortune! You have brought me nothing but good news—my head feels reeling—I can hardly grasp it all at once."

"Well, my dear boy, I am glad of it. For it seems to me that you and good news have been strangers for many a long day! And now, suppose we go in, and find out if your father is awake?"

CHAPTER XLV.
ONLY MR. JERVIS.

"I never saw such a change in any one!" faltered Mr. Pollitt, with some emotion, as he followed Mark out of his father's room. "He is years younger than I am, and he is so cadaverous and shrunken that he looks seventy at the very least. Poor fellow! he was in a desperate state at first, when he thought I had come to carry you off. I am glad you reassured him so completely. Well, as long as he is here, he shall have you. I understand matters now; I have seen with my own eyes, and one look is worth a ton of letters."

Mr. Pollitt was enchanted with his present quarters, with the great rambling house, its gardens, its situation, its quaint furniture. The solitude and silence were an extraordinary refreshment to the little world-worn cockney, after the roar of the London traffic, the throbbing of engines, and the rumbling of railway carriages.

In honour of the new arrival, the khansamah sent up a remarkably well-cooked dinner, not at all a jungle *menu*. There was excellent soup, fresh fish from a mountain "tal" (a lake), *entrées*, a brace of hill partridges, sweets, yellow cream, fruit, and black coffee. The claret was a still further agreeable surprise; it had been laid in by a connoisseur, and imported direct from Bordeaux *viâ* Pondicherry. But the greatest surprise of all was presented in the person of the host himself. With his heart warmed by sound old wine and the presence of a sound old friend, Major Jervis kindled up into a semblance of what he once had been. He talked connectedly and even brilliantly; he laughed and joked, and listened with unaffected delight to the history of Mr. Pollitt's journey and adventures *en route*. His eyes shone with something of their ancient fire; the lines and wrinkles seemed to fade from his face; his voice was that of a man who could still make himself heard on parade. Mr. Pollitt gazed and hearkened in blank amazement; he was entranced and carried away breathless by chronicles of hairbreadth escapes, tiger shooting, and elephant catching; by tales of Eastern superstitions, of lucky and unlucky horses, places, and people, stories of native life; of an English nobleman who lived in a bazaar, earning his bread by repairing carts and ekkas; of a young officer of good family and fortune, who had lost his head about a native girl, had abandoned his country, profession, and religion, and had adopted her people, and embraced her faith; how, in vain, his wealthy English relatives had besought him to return to them; how they had come out to seek him—had argued and implored, and finally prevailed on him to abandon his associates; and how, ere they had reached Bombay, they had lost him—he, unable to break the spell of the siren, had escaped back to his old haunts. He told of Englishmen who were lepers, living in sad solitude among the hills, unknown and nameless; of the burning of witches, of devil-worship, black magic, and human sacrifices. The most thrilling and extraordinary items of his past were unrolled as a scroll, and recapitulated in vivid and forcible language.

Who was this that held them spell-bound? thought his listeners. Not the shattered wreck of the forenoon, but the soldier who had seen much service, who had felt the pulse of events, who had absorbed India through his eyes and ears—*real* India, during a residence of thirty-five years in that mysterious, intoxicating, gorgeous land! Of frontier skirmishes, kept out of the newspapers, of friendly interchanges between foes in the field, of mysterious disappearances, of men who had laid down their lives for their country—heroes unknown to fame, whose deeds were unrecorded by one line of print, whose shallow graves were marked by rotting crosses on the bleak Afghan frontier.

Major Jervis kept his audience enthralled; even Mark's attention *rarely* wandered to a coolie who was at the moment running through the wooded hillsides by the light of the cold keen stars, with a letter in his loin-cloth addressed to "Miss Gordon."

It was one o'clock before the party dispersed; and as Major Jervis clapped his brother-in-law on the shoulder, with a hearty good night, he added—

"Who knows, Pollitt, but that I may be persuaded by your eloquence to go home with you, after all?"

"My father is very ill," said Mark, as he entered into his uncle's room at eight o'clock the next morning. "He wants to see you. I have been with him since six o'clock; and, Uncle Dan, I'm afraid that this is the end."

Yes, there was no doubt about that, thought Mr. Pollitt; death was surely written on the countenance that was turned to him. Last night had been the final flicker before the flame of life went out.

The invalid was propped up in a chair by a window looking towards the snows; but his face was ghastly, his breathing laboured.

"I'm glad you are here, Dan; glad we met once more." And he made a movement as if he would offer his wasted, helpless-looking hand. "You and Mark wanted me to go home," murmured the grey lips; "and I am going—sooner than you thought." He turned his dull eyes and fixed them intently on his son. "God bless you, Mark," he whispered almost inarticulately. These were his last words.

When Mr. Burgess arrived, an hour later, he was dead.

"Died of a failure of the heart's action, brought on by some overpowering excitement;" but, as far as he could judge, "under any circumstances he could not have outlived a week." Such was the missionary's verdict.

"Ah, sahib!" cried Mahomed, with up-raised hands and eyes, "I knew how it would be; there was the warning, the never-failing warning at twelve o'clock last night—*the voice*."

"What do you mean, Jan Mahomed?" Jervis returned quickly.

"The voice of a stranger, sahib, shouting in the yard. He was calling for his horse. He was going a long journey. Surely the Protector of the poor knows the truth of this? It is ever thus before a man's death—there is an order loudly spoken, 'Gorah tiar hye!'" ("Bring my horse!")

Major Jervis was laid in the cantonment cemetery the following morning. Mr. Burgess read the funeral service. Mark, Mr. Pollitt, and one or two neighbours assembled round the grave, whilst afar off stood servants, coolies, and many sick and poor, and lepers, to whom the "dear brother," now being laid to rest, had been a kind and generous friend.

Fernandez arrived, in answer to a telegram, full of joy, bustle, and importance. He could not understand the faces of the two Englishmen. It was, as he frankly stated, a happy release. He delighted in organization, change, and excitement, and undertook all arrangements with zeal. He seemed to be everywhere at once. He talked, strutted, gesticulated, and made such a stir that it seemed as if ten men had been added to the party.

"The house and land are Mark's," he explained to Mr. Pollitt; "not worth much," shrugging his shoulders. "Everything else comes to *me*—all the jewels. I wish I could show you those in the bank," and his eyes glittered as he thought of them. "But we will get out what is here and let you have a look at them, for they are native and very curious."

A big safe was accordingly unlocked, the contents brought forth and poured out, nay, heaped, upon a crimson-covered table, which displayed them to advantage.

Mr. Pollitt sat down deliberately, to examine what evidently represented an immense quantity of money, thus sunk in gold and precious stones. There were aigrettes of diamonds, the jewels dull and badly cut, but of extraordinarily great size. There were vases and boxes of gold, and white and green jade inlaid with rubies. Khas-dans, or betel boxes; jars for otto of roses; crescent ornaments for the turban, set with emeralds and diamonds; gold anklets, with the ends formed of elephant heads; forehead ornaments, set with great pearls with pendant drops; plumes or turahs for turbans, with strings of diamonds; armlets, bangles, rings for nose or ear, back-scratchers of gold and ivory, glorious ropes of pearls, and many huge unset emeralds and rubies. It was the collection and stores of generations, now about to be scattered to the four winds by the plump and restless hand of Fernandez Cardozo.

"I would like to give you something, Mark," he said, carelessly turning over piles of gold and precious stones as he spoke. "Will you accept a present from me, my good fellow?"

"Of course he will," said the little Londoner, with business-like promptitude.

"You joked with me about wearing a—a—necklace, eh, you remember, when I showed you a certain little bit of jewellery?" Fernandez looked conscious, and actually believed that he was blushing. "Well now, I am going to present *you* with one! Look at this!" holding towards him a string of large emeralds, pierced and run on a silken cord, and fastened off by a gold tassel. "These are for your future bride, Mark my boy."

"How did you know about her?" eyeing him gravely.

"Ho, ho, ho! Not a bad shot, I see! A bow drawn at a venture! Then there is such a young lady?"

"Yes," assented Mr. Pollitt, "and a very handsome young lady; you may take my word for *that*!"

"What is she like?" turning to Mark with sparkling eyes. "Fair or dark?"

"You shall see her some day, Fernandez. You must come to our wedding."

"I shall be most happy; but, my dear fellow, *do* describe her appearance. I am such a ladies' man, you know, such an admirer of beauty."

"Oh, she is tall, a head over you, Cardozo," said Mr. Pollitt, "and has dark hair, dark-grey eyes, and a very delicate colour, the air of a princess."

"Ah! then she shall have these pearls, instead of emeralds!" cried Fernandez with enthusiasm, plunging his fat fingers into ropes of the former, and holding them aloft for inspection. Four rows of large pearls fastened off by a quaint old clasp, and a little tassel of rubies.

"They are far too valuable—it is much too handsome a gift," objected Mark, holding back instinctively.

"Nothing is too handsome for a handsome girl! and, for the matter of value, the emeralds, though they look like so many balls of green glass, beat them! If you refuse them in her name, I assure you I shall be quite affronted; and, surely, it is only right that the major's daughter should have one small gift from amid all the begum's jewels."

"I do not call that a small gift, Fernandez, and I am very much obliged to you; but I will take it to Miss Gordon, and, later on, she will thank you personally."

"They are superb!" exclaimed Mr. Pollitt, rapturously. "I shall give her diamonds—to correspond."

Incongruous pair though they were, Mr. Pollitt and Mr. Cardozo hit it off surprisingly well. Fernandez's florid manner, Oriental ideas, and ornamental language interested the hard-headed matter-of-fact little Englishman. They walked and smoked and argued noisily together, whilst Mark rode away to visit a certain newly-made grave, and to take leave of the Persian lady.

"Ah, my friend, I have been waiting for you," she said, rising from the chabootra, or band-stand. "I thought you would surely come to say farewell. Of course you are going away?"

"Yes. I am going away immediately."

"And you will marry her—now—and gain your heart's desire?"

"I hope so. And I am come to offer you what may fulfil yours!"

She stared at him with an air of almost fierce inquiry.

"It is the Yellow House. Will you accept it, for your lifetime? You said you wished for a large bungalow in a central position—and there you are!"

"The Yellow House! Oh, it is too much. No, I could not take it, not even for my poor. No, no, no!" and she shook her head with an air of decision.

"Why not?" he argued; "it is mine to do with as I will; and there is nothing that will give me greater pleasure than to feel that it is in your hands—and the means of doing good—instead of standing closed, empty, and falling into ruins. There is the garden for the patients to walk in, the grazing for cows, the big rooms for wards. I will thankfully pay an apothecary and assistant, and whatever is necessary."

"You wish to establish a sort of hill hospital for the poor in these parts?" inquired the Persian, incredulously.

"Nay; you have already done that. I only ask leave to help you. If you will not accept the Pela Kothi from me, take it from—us both—or from Honor. You will not refuse her!"

"And shall I never see you again—or her?" she faltered.

"Who can say? Perhaps one day we may come and visit you. At any rate, she will write to you."

"But how can she write to me—a—a—Persian woman?" looking at him with an intensity that was not pleasant to contemplate.

"At least, *I* shall write to you," he rejoined, slightly disconcerted. "I will send you a certain yearly sum to spend on the wretched lepers, and in any charitable form that you may think best. Mr. Burgess will translate my letters for you, and also any answers that you may be good enough to send me. We do not wish to lose sight of you, if we can help it."

"*We!* how soon you have learnt to say it! You are so happy, where you have hitherto known great misery, and the poor native woman will soon have passed from your mind. You are released. I shall never be released—but by death. You will be in another world—you, and the Miss Sahib! Will you give her this from me? It is a little charm. Nay, do not laugh. What am I but an ignorant, superstitious native? Nevertheless, I mean well. This is an amulet against sickness, poverty, or the loss of friends; an old hill woman gave it to me. She said it never failed. I have no friends to lose, but I am a stranger to poverty and sickness."

"I will give it to her to-morrow," taking from her hand a smooth dark-green stone, about the size of a filbert. "As to having no friends, may Miss Gordon and I not call ourselves your friends?"

"How can an English lady, and an English sahib, be the friends of—a woman of my people?" she inquired, with a face as expressionless as a mask.

"It shall be as you will," he answered gravely. "But I see nothing to stand between us. Remember that we wish to be your friends, if you will have us. And now I'm afraid I must go."

He saw her lips quiver, as she suddenly turned away her face, and dismissed him with a quick imperious gesture.

Ere he left the valley he looked back once. The Persian was standing precisely where he had left her. In answer to his farewell signal, she waved a handkerchief—and thus involuntarily betrayed herself. It was the action of an Englishwoman!

Mr. Pollitt was actually reluctant to abandon this life of pastoral simplicity. The fragrant garden, the clear exhilarating air, the sturdy simple hill folk, the view of hill and plains, steeped in a blue or violet haze, appeared to hold him fast. He and Fernandez agreed to travel together in a leisurely comfortable fashion; but Mark would not and could not wait. He was in love. Where love exists, it is the only thing in life—all else is nothing. He laid a dâk of his three ponies on the road, and, early one afternoon, galloped off to Shirani, with two wedding presents in his pocket.

Perhaps the grey and bay ponies were as anxious as their rider to return to their former haunts; at any rate, the forty miles which lay between the Pela Kothi and Rookwood were accomplished at a pace that has never yet been approached, and as the result of this rapid travelling, Mark Jervis arrived a considerable time before he was expected. That evening Lady Brande had been entertaining a dinner-party, one of her most superior "burra-khanas." People had left the table and were assembled in the drawing-room, where it was generally noted that Miss Gordon was looking brilliantly handsome. Yes, she had entirely recovered her looks. A few months ago she had gone off most terribly; but that queer hushed-up love affair of hers had been quite enough to blanch her face and waste away her flesh. Some one was at the piano singing a penetrating Italian love song, when it became evident that an exceedingly late guest was on the point of arrival. There was the flash of a lantern outside, the stamping of ponies' hoofs, and the sound of a manly voice that set Honor's heart beating.

Sir Pelham slipped away for a moment, and then returned and glanced significantly at his wife.

She rose at once, and hurried out of the room, and was seen through the open verandah in animated conversation with a young fellow in riding dress. Etiquette forbade Honor—the most concerned—to move. Propriety chained her hand and foot.

"I hope you will excuse me," panted Lady Brande, returning somewhat breathless, and addressing her guests, in a voice between laughing and crying. "He declares that he is not fit to appear. He has just come back.—It is only Mr. Jervis!"

CHAPTER XLVI.
A WEDDING WITH TWO CAKES.

The following is a portion of a letter from a lady in Shirani, to her dearest friend on the plains:—

"It is true that you have the hideous journey over, all the packing, getting off of carts, paying farewell calls, and nasty little bills, and that you are settled on the plains in winter quarters—all this misery is before me. Nevertheless I think you took up your winter quarters prematurely. October is quite my month in the hills, the air is so crisp and clear, you can see for miles, the Autumn tints are exquisite, and the low country seems veiled in a wash, of the most exquisite cobalt and amethyst tints.

"Moreover, I have been here for *the* wedding. You want to know all about it, of course, and I will do as I would be done by, and begin at the very beginning. When young Jervis unexpectedly returned, every one was quite vulgarly astounded; the explanation of his absence was perfectly simple, and he brought in his train, his uncle—the rich man—the real, true, and only millionaire! And of course they stayed at Rookwood, and Miss Gordon's engagement was given out at once—I must say the pair looked delightfully happy. I used to meet them riding about the pine roads, they also came down to the club, and tennis, and actually behaved like reasonable people, and a great deal less like lovers (in public), than other couples who were not engaged. Lady Brande was simply one large smile whenever you saw her, and indeed she and the withered little millionaire were preposterously radiant. He was delighted with everything he saw. (A complete contrast to some of our visitors from home.) Among other things, he appears to be particularly pleased with his future niece; I have noticed them constantly together—in fact, I think he monopolized her rather more than was fair. Lady Brande and the nephew have always been *au mieux*! At first there was an awful rumour that owing to a recent affliction in the bridegroom's family—the death of his father—the wedding was to be very quiet—bride to be married in her habit, and to go away from the church. But, after all, a compromise was effected—in deference to Lady Brande's wishes. There was to be no band, no grand breakfast, no fuss—in deference to the young man's wishes; but the bride was to have an orthodox white gown, and any one who pleased might come to the church and see them married, and afterwards adjourn to Rookwood for cake and champagne. Needless to tell you, that every one pleased to attend the only wedding of the season, and a wedding that had an air of romance about it, and was certainly a love match. The presents were really tokens of good will—not given for show, and were 'numerous and costly,' as they say in the papers; the handsomest, in my opinion, was a splendid necklace of rows of pearls, most quaint. One of the smallest was a buttonhook from Mrs. Langrishe. I don't know *how* she can be so mean! I believe she was very urgent in pressing Lady Brande to take some of her preparations for that other wedding off her hands. And Lady B., who is the soul of good nature, was forced into purchasing the wedding cake, never unpacked—she had a superb one, of course, from Pelitis; but this she bought as a supplementary affair for cutting up afterwards and sending away.

"Sweet Primrose and Dolly Merton were the little bridesmaids; and as the former insisted on having 'a gentleman to walk with,' Mrs. Paul's two handsome boys, in white page suits, accompanied the pair of small maids. They made the prettiest quartette—Dolly and Sweet in such smart frocks, Sweet looking really like a young angel, with her golden hair. However, she came out in her true colours before the end of the day. I wondered that she was invited to be present in any form, but Miss Gordon said that Mr. Jervis particularly wished it. There is no accounting for tastes—of course he does not *know* her. I declare to you, that child strutted up the aisle, in her white silk shoes and stockings, as if she were spurning criticism, and as if the whole packed church full of people were assembled solely to gaze at Sweet Primrose! There were several outsiders present—friends the bridegroom had picked up—two or three young planters, whose hair wanted cutting badly, a missionary with an immense brown beard, who took part in the ceremony, that funny Mr. Cardozo, who seemed all teeth and diamond rings. The bride wore a lovely plain white satin and *the* pearls. She was rather nervous; but the bridegroom was perfectly composed. They looked so triumphantly happy coming down the aisle arm-in-arm. After all, there is nothing like a love match!

"We assembled in immense force at Rookwood, to drink the health of the newly-married couple. Sir Pelham made a capital speech—neat, brief, and witty. There were one or two unofficial remarks which may be recorded; for example, Colonel Sladen said, 'She came up with him—a case of the early bird. The first day she was brought to the club I gave her a piece of sound advice—I told her to keep her eye on the millionaire. Though I had got hold of the wrong end of the stick, it appears that she had *not*!'

"But it was generally acknowledged that Sweet Primrose made *the* speech of the occasion! fortunately it was to a comparatively small audience. As she sat stuffing herself with almond paste, she suddenly announced, in that shrill little pipe of hers, '*This is Miss Paske's wedding-cake!*' And Mrs. Langrishe, who was sitting close by, looked as if she was about to faint, and no wonder. Of course it was not Miss Paske's wedding-cake; but the prying elf, who had been to Rookwood the previous day, whilst her mother was examining the presents, had overheard certain whisperings, and, having a particular eye for *cake*, had noted cake number two. Mrs. Sladen almost threw herself on the child, and managed to silence her and stifle her terrible tongue; but I believe the imp actually exacted a solemn promise that she was to have a large sample of what she pleasantly called '*the other one*' at the very earliest opportunity.

"None of this by-play came to the eyes or ears of the wedding party, and soon we were all on the *qui vive* to speed the bride. There was a great deal of kissing, but no tears. The happy pair were accompanied by a white dog, and drove off (quite a new departure) in a smart victoria, which was almost buried in slippers. If slippers are any sign of good feeling, they are the most popular couple that were married here for years. I don't believe that there is one single old shoe to be found in the whole of Shirani."

THE END.

Milton Keynes UK
Ingram Content Group UK Ltd.
UKHW011123180424
441376UK00004B/190